THE MOST DANGEROUS MAN IN THE WEST . . .

Stillman's ey[...]ng at the sky. His [...]d as his vision clea[...]ying on the ground [...]g himself out of the saddle.

Sudden pain stabbed through his side. He groaned, wincing at the fire that spread across his rib cage, and his forehead beaded with sweat. His hand went to his side and came away wet with blood.

He realized he had been shot. But against all odds, he was still alive. Alive to fight another day. Tomorrow or the next day, it did not matter.

Time was nothing to a man left for dead.

TENBOW

MATT BRAUN

St. Martin's Paperbacks

TENBOW

Copyright © 1991 by Matt Braun.

ISBN: 0-312-93817-9
EAN: 9780312-93817-8

Printed in the United States of America

Signet Paperbacks edition / February 1991
St. Martin's Paperbacks edition / January 2006

St. Martin's Paperbacks are published by St. Martin's Press, 175 Fifth Avenue, New York, NY 10010.

10 9 8 7 6 5 4 3 2 1

To

Alan and Janet

friends and more for all seasons

TENBOW

ONE

The hunter held his horse to a slow walk. There was no reason for speed, and he was concerned that undue noise might spook his quarry. His stalk had been cautious and hidden, nothing to betray his presence. He felt assured of a kill.

Sunlight filtered through a thick stand of aspen, covering the mountainside in dappled shadow. He reined to a halt near the crest and stepped down from the saddle. With some care he tied his horse to a tree, looping the reins into a snug knot. Gunfire startled even the best of horses, and he'd learned long ago not to risk being left afoot. The mountains were rough traveling on shank's mare.

From his saddlebags he removed a parfleche of tanned leather. Inside were strips of hardened jerky, made from elk meat. A week past, under a hot June sun, he had cured the meat until it was dark and brittle. After taking a wrinkled strip from the parfleche, he returned the leather pouch to his saddlebags. He broke off a hunk with strong teeth, allowing saliva to soften the jerky, and stood chewing without haste. He still had time to spare, and the thought of a kill always summoned his hunger. He savored the gamy taste, partial to sun-cured elk.

Afterward, he licked his fingers and wiped them dry on his buckskin shirt. He was a large man, with shaggy black hair and a thick beard flecked with gray. He wore a battered hat and trousers stuffed into moccasin boots favored by the northern tribes. Strapped around his waist was a gun belt with a holstered Colt .44 and a honed skinning knife. The buckskin shirt was stained with grease and sweat, and crisscrossed over his shoulders was a wide belt filled with rifle cartridges. He looked like a man of the wild, fully able to survive off the land.

Hunger satisfied, he was ready now for the hunt. He pulled a Sharps .50-90 from the saddle scabbard and checked to make sure the hammer was down. Then he walked uphill, leaving the horse standing hip-shot in the sunlight. From years of habit, he moved quietly through the aspens, avoiding the telltale snap of twigs and branches underfoot. At the crest, he paused, scouting ahead, still in no hurry. He scanned the terrain beyond the forward slope.

Some distance to the west, the Wind River range jutted skyward. A vast stretch in the Rocky Mountain chain, the peaks angled northwestward through Wyoming Territory. Eastward, between the taller summits and the mountainous woodlands bordered by the Wind River, lay Tenbow Valley. To the direct front, north from where the hunter paused, there was a high country meadowland. A stream snaked across the grassy swale and disappeared through a canyon bounded by steep hills. Three cows and a spring-born calf stood grazing near a bend in the stream.

The hunter moved forward. Halfway down the slope, the heavy stand of aspens splayed outward in a V-shaped formation. He again paused, scanning the wings of the open V in the timber. The natural clearing, which spread wider as it dropped off downhill, provided a broad field of fire. To the trained eye, the range from the notch in the aspens to the cows appeared to be slightly more than four hundred yards. Good shooting distance.

After a moment, the hunter walked to the edge of the treeline. He selected a shady spot beneath the canopy of an aspen and sat down. At the base of the tree, the ground was relatively flat, and he shifted his rump until he found a comfortable position. With his knees bent, he dug his heels into the earth and braced his hindquarters against the trunk of the tree. Hefting the rifle, he raised the leaf sight at the rear and set the crossbar for the proper range. He then propped his elbows on his knees, snugged the butt of the rifle into his shoulder, and sighted on the cows. Hold a tad high and it looked to be a perfect downhill shot.

Grunting to himself, he lowered the rifle, levered the trigger guard, and opened the breech. He slipped a massive shell from the cartridge belt, inserted it into the breech, and jacked the lever upward. The big Sharps was designed to hurl a slug nearly a half inch in diameter, punched onward by a formidable load of powder. The heavy octagonal barrel made it a weighty piece, but it was deadly accurate up to ranges of six hundred yards. The wallop of the broad-nosed fifty slug was guaranteed to down man or beast. One shot, one kill.

A lazy white butterfly floated past on a gentle updraft. The hunter watched it idly, reminded that he hadn't yet checked the wind. He pulled a tuft of dry grass from the ground and tossed it overhead. The grass drifted a hair to the left and settled slowly at his feet. He made a mental note to hold a hair to the right when he sighted, and allow for the slight shift in windage. That, along with a smidgen high, would make it a clean, dead-center shot. One he'd made a hundred times or more during his years in the mountains. Today, like all those other times, would be a simple exercise of skill. Pick a spot and touch off a tack-driver.

The hunter's every instinct was suddenly alerted. A horseman on a chestnut gelding emerged from the mouth of the canyon. Gazing down from the mountainside, the hunter studied man and mount, satisfied that he'd selected the right spot. From the old days to the present, he had spent nearly thirty years in the Wind Rivers and the Tetons. He knew every ridge and valley as though mapped in his head, and he had outguessed bear and elk and deer beyond count. Today he'd outguessed a man.

The horseman's name was Bud Ledbetter. He owned a small outfit headquartered on the Middle Fork of the Popo Agie River. He had a wife and three kids, and five cowhands who hired on during roundup and the trailing season. His was a hardscrabble operation, with a herd seldom topping a thousand head, strictly hand-to-mouth from one season to the next. He owed the banker in Tenbow everything but his soul, certainly more than his stock and his land were worth. One bad winter would put him out of the cow business.

The hunter knew all these things and more about Bud Ledbetter. For the past week he had scouted Ledbetter's operation, observing the daily routine from a distance. He knew the rancher arose before dawn and went to bed an hour or so after supper. He knew that shortly after sunrise Ledbetter and the hands would ride out for the day's work. Of greater importance, he knew the rancher believed in one man for one job. Watchful, he'd noted that Ledbetter seldom teamed the hands while gathering strays. The men were each assigned a section of the canyons and meadows where cows had scattered during the winter. And Ledbetter set the example, working as hard as his men. He always took a section for himself.

Ever cautious, the hunter had trailed Ledbetter for a week. Like the rancher, he believed that work well done was work that left no loose ends. No one had seen him, and no one suspected he was tracking Bud Ledbetter. For all practical purposes, he was an invisible presence, stalking unwary game. Which was what separated a hunter from the hunted. Deliberate and unhurried, watchful and patient, avoiding all risks. The outcome was what mattered, a tidy end to the job. Done right, his quarry never heard the shot.

Early that morning, while the stars were still out, he'd left his camp deep in the mountains. By dawn he was secreted in a grove of trees overlooking the ranch compound. As sunrise lighted the land, he observed Ledbetter gather the men outside the corral and tick off their assignments for the day. Then, as they rode out in different directions, he had trailed the rancher at a safe distance. Within the hour he'd known where Ledbetter was headed, a mountain meadow at the end of a forested canyon. From there it was a simple matter to circle around on the high ground, shortcut the ride. Ten minutes later he was positioned and waiting, hidden beneath the aspens.

Watchful now, he admired the way Ledbetter approached the cows. The mama cow and her calf made a spirited run for the west end of the meadow. But Ledbetter swung wide, spurring his gelding, and hazed them back along the creek. Some moments later the three cows and the calf were again bunched together. Like any good cattleman, Ledbetter never ran the fat off his cows. He pushed them instead at a fast walk, toward the mouth of the canyon. Once they were moving he reined to a halt, took out the makings, and rolled himself a cigarette. He dug a match from his shirt pocket.

The hunter shouldered his rifle. He eared back the hammer and squinted over the sights, holding high and a hair right. He took a deep breath, then exhaled, and gently squeezed the trigger. The Sharps boomed just as Ledbetter struck the match on his thumbnail. An instant later the big fifty slug whacked him in the chest,

exploded his heart, and exited on a downward
angle with a spray of blood. The chestnut gelding skittered sideways and Ledbetter toppled
headfirst out of the saddle. He hit the ground
having never heard the shot. Arms and legs
akimbo, he lay facedown, unmoving.

Echoing off the mountains, the reverberation
of the gunshot was like rolling thunder. The
gelding and the cows, spooked by the rumbling sound, pounded across the meadow and
vanished into the canyon. A long moment
passed while the hunter sat staring at the
rancher's body. Finally satisfied that the hunt
was ended, he rose to his feet. After ejecting the
spent shell, he turned and walked off through
the aspens.

On the back slope of the mountain, the
hunter jammed the Sharps into its scabbard.
He unhitched his horse from the tree and
stepped into the saddle. As he rode off, the
thought occurred that it might be days before
the body was found. By then, what had happened here today would be a part of his past.
For he would have begun another hunt.

And then another, until the job was done.

TWO

The morning ritual never varied. Stillman always awoke fully alert, prepared to get on with the day's business. He might have dreamt, but dreams were part of sleep, seldom remembered. His thoughts centered instead on the here and now.

Bright sunlight streamed through the windows. He rolled out of bed and padded barefoot to the washstand. He poured water from a pitcher into the basin and scrubbed his face with both hands. Still dripping, he dipped a shaving brush in the tepid water, sloshed it around in a soap mug, and lathered his face. After stropping his razor, he shaved with quick, steady strokes. Then, switching to a small pair of scissors, he trimmed his brushy mustache.

The face in the mirror scarcely held his attention. So long as he was reasonably well-groomed, he rarely gave any thought to his looks one way or another. What he was born with was what he had, and he'd always been one to make do. The nose was a bit off-center, broken a couple of times, and there was a ridged scar over one eyebrow. But those were vestiges of the trade, all part of his work. He prided himself that those were the only signs. On occasion he reminded himself that he'd been shot at, but never shot.

Finished shaving, he moved to a standing wardrobe with double mirrors. The compartment on the right side was filled with assorted suits, some conservative and some flashy, none of which seemed in character for the man who called himself Jack Stillman. He opened the door on the left side and selected whipcord trousers, a linsey shirt, and a corduroy jacket. High-topped cowman's boots completed the outfit, and after dressing, he moved back to the bed. Hanging on the bedpost was a holstered Colt .45 with a lustrous blue finish and dulled ivory grips. He strapped it around his waist with practiced ease.

On the way out the door he took a flat-crowned Stetson from a hat tree. In the hall he turned and walked toward the stairwell. For the past eight years he had maintained quarters at the Cattlemen's House, one of the better hotels in Cheyenne. He preferred the hotel to a boardinghouse, where resident busybodies allowed a man no privacy. Here he could come and go as he pleased, with no one the wiser. A man in his trade disliked snoopers and gadflies, people with an inordinate interest in another fellow's business. The less known about his work, the better.

Downstairs, he swapped greetings with the desk clerk and crossed the lobby. Cattle season was in full swing and cowmen from around the territory were clustered in the lobby, talking and laughing. Some of them nodded to him, and others grew quiet, avoiding his gaze. Those who looked away were ranchers with large spreads, members of the International Cattlemen's Association. For all practical purposes, they controlled politics in Wyoming Territory and were a law unto themselves. He refused to work for men who set their own standards of justice, and they resented his attitude. He returned the favor.

Inside the dining room, he took a seat at a window table. The hour was late, going on eight o'clock, and most of the tables were empty. Cattlemen were early risers, and during the season he made it a point to come downstairs after the breakfast rush. That way he managed a leisurely meal without the room turning silent and men darting hidden glances in his direction. For all their hostility, the large ranchers nonetheless respected him and were careful never to give offense. He'd killed too many men for them to behave otherwise. The problem, though unspoken, was that he wouldn't kill for hire.

"Good morning to you, Jack."

Stillman looked up as a waitress approached the table. Her name was Molly Adair and she was a saucy lass with the blush of an Irish rose in her cheeks. Her red hair and blue eyes only served to accentuate the ripe curves of her figure. She enjoyed a running flirtation with the hotel's resident manhunter.

"Morning, Molly," Stillman replied. "You're looking mighty fine today."

"Listen to him!" she said, rolling her china blue eyes. "You'd turn a girl's head with your fancy talk."

"Maybe you're the girl."

"Am I, indeed?" She laughed, posing with one hand on her hip. "You've yet to show me it's so."

"Guess I'm just slow," Stillman said, smiling. "Wouldn't want to rush into anything."

"God love us," she said with mock indignation. "You're not slow, you're deaf!"

"C'mon, Molly, when you talk, I'm all ears."

She knew it wasn't true. Talk around town was that he kept regular company with a young widow. Yet a girl could always hope, and the thought of him in her bed made her skin tingle. She laughed, shook her head.

"Well, enough of that," she said. "What'll it be today—the owlhoot special?"

"Not today," Stillman said, matching her smile. "How about buckwheat cakes and ham?"

"And a pot of coffee?"

"Molly, you're a born mind reader."

She turned away, wig-wagging her hips as she walked toward the kitchen. Stillman's gaze shifted from her admirable rump to the window. He stared out at the street, hearing again her reference to the "owlhoot special." She'd spoken in jest, but there was truth in humor. His reputation as a manhunter was a matter of record. Outlaws, men on the owlhoot, were his stock in trade.

The Union Pacific had selected Cheyenne as its western headquarters in 1867. At the time, Jack Stillman had been serving as a special agent with the railroad. His work as a railroad detective, and several shoot-outs with train robbers, brought him a modicum of fame. A year later he was appointed deputy U.S. marshal, and his reputation as a manhunter began in earnest. On one occasion, operating in disguise, he had entered Hole-in-the-Wall, the outlaw sanctuary, and emerged to tell the tale. No other lawman had ever duplicated the feat.

In 1870, he had traded his federal badge for a

lucrative job with the Overland Stage. For six years, working as the company's chief detective, he had pursued stage robbers throughout the western territories. According to the newspapers, since his arrival in Wyoming, he had killed upward of eleven outlaws. The true number was never known, for he'd refused all comment on the matter. Finally, at the urging of several prominent businessmen, he had established his own detective agency. Over the past two years he'd operated as an undercover investigator, adopting a different disguise for each job. His client list included banks, mining companies, several railroads, and an occasional assignment for the stage line. A recent article in the *Police Gazette*, dated June 1878, had dubbed him the most feared manhunter on the Western frontier.

Stillman found himself uncomfortable with the notoriety. Staring out the window, sipping a final cup of coffee, he reflected on the vagaries of his profession. Articles in newspapers and various periodicals had brought him prominence and a growing list of clients. But those same articles were read by thieves and robbers, which kept him uppermost in their minds. Even worse, an old tintype photo taken when he had been a deputy marshal regularly accompanied stories in the newspapers. To him, the photo was much on the order of a wanted poster. He could easily imagine it tacked on the walls of outlaw dens across the territory.

Under the best of circumstances, working undercover was a dicey proposition. But now, with his mug plastered on the pages of newspapers, the job had become doubly difficult. All that saved him was a certain talent for disguise, and the gift for adopting a role, much as an actor plays a part on stage. Otherwise, he would have been long dead and buried, gunned down by some hard-case who read the newspapers. Yet the game was part of the lure, the challenge that he risked his life on every assignment. He took pride in his craft, and danger somehow invigorated him, kept him on his toes. Outwitting the tough nuts of the world was an intoxicant, almost addictive.

A last swig of coffee ended his rumination. He left money on the table, waved to Molly, and headed for the door. Time to get on with the day's business.

Outside, Stillman paused on the hotel veranda. Several cattlemen and stock buyers were seated in rockers, and some of them went silent, staring at him. Taking his time, he extracted a cheroot from his coat pocket and lit up in a haze of smoke. Then he stepped off the veranda and turned downtown.

Stillman never ceased to be amazed by the

beehive of activity on the streets. In the past few years he'd seen Cheyenne grow from a ramshackle crossroads to a bustling plains metropolis. As the capital of Wyoming Territory, with a population of nearly twenty thousand, it was now a center of commerce and the major western railhead. On the south side, bordering the railroad tracks, gambling dens and dance halls, variety theaters and bawdy houses, composed a thriving vice district. Farther uptown, the business district was packed with stores and hotels, saloons and restaurants, several banks, and the state capitol building. For good reason, Cheyenne was known as the Magic City of the Plains.

Yet for all its growth, Cheyenne remained a curious admixture of cowtown and citified elegance. The Union Pacific had transformed it into a hub of trade, an ever-expanding business and financial center. As the territorial capital, frequented by lawmakers and wealthy power brokers, the city had slowly assumed an aura of respectability and cultivation. At the same time it was the central railhead and shipment point for Wyoming's vast cattle industry.

Every summer herds were trailed into Cheyenne from ranches all across the High Plains. After being sold to cattle brokers, the cows were shipped east for slaughter. A great deal of money exchanged hands, and in the process the town prospered. However progressive, everyone from the governor to storekeepers catered to cattlemen for the most basic of reasons. Cows were big business, the mainstay of Cheyenne's economic growth.

Centered around the train depot were various enterprises related to the cattle trade. The vice district, where a carnival atmosphere prevailed during trailing season, was devoted exclusively to the rough tastes of cowhands. Nearby were the holding pens and loading yards, along with several livestock dealers. Horses, trailed overland from Texas, were yet another flourishing business. Wyoming cattlemen found it easier to buy than breed, and thereby created a market. Good saddle mounts were in constant demand.

Stillman's office was a block north of the train depot. There, in the town's original bank building, he maintained a one-room cubbyhole on the second floor. As he approached the entrance, a newsboy wandered past and he bought the morning paper. A voice interrupted him before he had a chance to check the headlines:

"How you been, Jack?"

Harry Crocker, superintendent of the rail yards, stepped from the street onto the boardwalk. They were old friends, dating back to the time Stillman had served as a special agent for the railroad. Crocker halted in front of him and they exchanged a handshake.

"Where you been hiding?" Stillman asked. "I haven't seen you around."

"Hell's bells," Crocker grumbled. "Trailin' season's here, and you know what that means. I'm up to my ass in cows."

"I hear it's gonna be a good year."

"More'n likely a record year. Them people back east just can't get enough beef."

Stillman nodded. "Guess that ought to make the Cattlemen's Association happy."

"Like pigs in mud." Crocker studied him a moment. "You still on the outs with them?"

"I'm choosy who I work for, Harry."

Crocker wasn't surprised by the statement. Apart from his reputation with a gun, Stillman was known as a man who brooked nonsense from no one. A solid six-footer, he was lean and tough, thick through the shoulders. His features were pleasant enough, with a square jaw and wide brow and a thatch of light chestnut hair. Yet his eyes, curiously impersonal, gave other men pause. His gaze was not so much cold as stoic, somehow detached. Not a man to cross, for any reason.

"How's business?" Crocker said, changing the subject. "Workin' on a hot case, are you?"

"Not just now," Stillman admitted. "Seems like everybody's gone to ground for the summer. Almost makes you wish someone would rob a train."

"Judas Priest!" Crocker barked. "Don't even think such a thing. You're liable to give somebody ideas."

"Only a joke, Harry."

"Yeah, but it ain't no laughin' matter."

"No, I reckon not," Stillman said, smiling. "Specially if you work for the Union Pacific."

Crocker laughed, and they parted after a handshake. Stillman crossed the boardwalk and took the outside stairs of the bank building. On the second floor, four offices were situated along a central hallway. Lawyers occupied the first two and a land surveyor worked out of the third. Stillman's office was at the end of the hall, on the street side. A frosted-glass panel on the door bore a neat hand-lettered sign.

JOHN STILLMAN
INVESTIGATIONS

Stillman unlocked the door. The interior was as spartan as a monk's cell. An ancient desk was positioned near the window, with a tattered leather chair behind it and two wooden armchairs in front. A row of file cabinets was wedged against the wall flanking the desk. He crossed the room and took a seat in the squeaky leather chair.

Unfolding the newspaper, he scanned the front page. A story caught his eye about the Lincoln County War, currently big news out of New Mexico Territory. According to the report, a pint-sized desperado known as Billy the Kid was killing people in droves. For a moment, Stillman considered wiring the authorities in New Mexico and offering his services. Or maybe suggest that they export Billy the Kid to Wyoming. The idea was improbable but appealing, the offspring of boredom. Things were dull as dirt without an active case.

A knock sounded at the door. Stillman folded the newspaper and dropped it on the desk. "C'mon in," he called out, "it's open."

The door swung inward and a man dressed in his Sunday suit stepped into the office. He was on the sundown side of forty, with windseamed features and hands gnarled from rough work. All that, along with his high-crowned hat, told the tale. He was a cattleman decked out for a trip to town.

"Howdy," he said, closing the door. "Are you Jack Stillman, the detective?"

"One and the same," Stillman replied. "What can I do for you?"

"I'm Carl Richter, from Tenbow Valley. I'd like to talk to you on a confidential matter."

"Have a seat." Stillman waited until he'd taken a chair. "I recollect Tenbow's over on the Wind River range. You're a long ways from home."

"Well, you see," Richter said with a shrug, "we don't have any detectives out that direction."

"From your rig, I take you as a cattleman. Maybe you've heard, I'm not on a sociable terms with the Association."

"The Association be damned!" Richter said hotly. "I'm here to talk about murder—four murders!"

Richter went on to tell a chilling story. Within the last month a reign of terror had settled over Tenbow Valley. Three small ranchers and a homesteader had been killed from ambush, shot at long range with a rifle. The county sheriff, after investigating the murders, had come away thoroughly stumped. The killer never left a trace. No tracks, no leads. Nothing.

"What's it to you?" Stillman said when he had finished. "You got a stake in this somehow?"

"From the looks of things," Richter observed, "there'll be more killing. I figure I'm on the list."

"How so?"

"I own a good-sized spread. Way I see it, that makes me a target."

"You saying you suspect somebody?"

"Yeah, I do."

"Tell me about it."

Richter expressed the belief that the murders were part of a sinister plot engineered by one of two men. The first was Will Sontag, an old cattle baron who once claimed all of Tenbow Valley as his domain. The second was Frank Devlin, an aggressive land speculator new to the valley. After every murder Devlin had been johnny-on-the-spot, offering to buy out the widow.

"I've got no proof," he concluded, "but they're both a sorry lot. Either one could be behind it."

Stillman looked interested. "Are you asking me to take the case?"

"Wouldn't be here if I wasn't."

"I don't work cheap," Stillman said. "Twenty a day and expenses. And you're hiring me, not my gun."

"Agreed," Richter said quickly. "You just catch the bastard. We'll see to it he's hung legal."

"One last thing," Stillman told him. "Nobody knows about our arrangement. Mum's the word, or I don't take the job."

Richter frowned. "How'll I know what's happening?"

"You won't," Stillman said bluntly. "I'll contact you when there's something to report. Till then you don't know me."

"Whatever you say."

Richter paid him a hundred dollars in advance. Then they shook hands on it and the cattleman walked from the office. After the door closed, Stillman returned to his chair. He leaned back, his face creased in a thoughtful expression.

Four men murdered and two suspects. Not that Richter's suspicions were anything more than hot air. He'd learned long ago that nothing was what it appeared on the surface. All the same, it was a place to start.

He began thinking about Tenbow Valley.

THREE

Later that morning, Stillman headed uptown. After considerable thought he'd decided on a cover story for the assignment. Once in Tenbow, he would then play it fast and loose. Anybody, train robber or mad-dog killer, could be caught. All it took was persistence, and a few breaks.

Yet it never paid to rush a manhunt. What he knew about Tenbow and the killings was essentially what Carl Richter had told him. Maybe that was the whole story, and then again, maybe there was more. Word about such things always got around, particularly among peace officers. He knew just the man to ask.

The territorial capitol was located on the outskirts of the business district. There, at the rear of the building, the federal government occupied several offices. The largest, and certainly the busiest, was the office of the U.S. marshal.

The outer room contained desks for four deputies and two clerks and an impressive array of file cabinets. Federal crime was a full-time business in Wyoming.

Stillman was an infrequent visitor. But his relationship with the deputies was one of trust and mutual respect. As a former lawman, he was one of the breed, a member of the club. Moreover, they admired him as a man who had few equals in a tight situation. For his part, he knew from experience that theirs was a difficult and thankless job. The pay was small, the hours were long, and most of their time was spent in the saddle. Which was the reason they were called Horseback Marshals.

Thomas Walker, the head marshal, rode a desk chair. Contrary to popular thought, the position of U.S. Marshal was a political appointment. The majority of men selected for the job had never worn a badge. Their political connections rather than their credentials as a peace officer were the deciding factor. Someone with clout in Washington suggested a name, and the president signed the commission papers. The patronage system, hard at work, performed the baptismal on yet another quasi-lawman.

Stillman had resigned for that very reason. After two years as a deputy, he'd concluded that politics was a distasteful business. Discretion and tact, and a talent for ass-kissing, were prerequisites for advancement. His sometimes abrupt manner, coupled with the impulse to call a spade a spade, were not the mark of a diplomat. Gradually, though he'd made his mark as a lawman, it became apparent that he would never be appointed U.S. Marshal. So he had quit and ultimately found the line of work that suited him best. A private investigator, particularly one with brass balls, could call anyone a son of a bitch.

For all that, he nonetheless respected Tom Walker. The man was mentally sharp, a good administrator, and he'd never broken his word. What he didn't know about tracking down cutthroats and thieves would fill a tome. But he gave his deputies plenty of leeway, as well as the credit for a job that was both dirty and dangerous. Unknown to anyone else, he also employed Stillman from time to time on sensitive assignments. These were active cases that his deputies had failed to solve, and were therefore treated with great secrecy. Stillman was paid from a slush fund and the marshal's office was credited with clearing a difficult case. Everyone benefited by the arrangement.

The inner office, furnished to Walker's taste, was a showcase of walnut and leather. One of the clerks ushered Stillman inside and gently closed the door. Walker came around his desk, hand outstretched, with a beaming smile.

"Well, Jack," he said affably. "What a coincidence. I was about to send for you."

"Saved you the trouble," Stillman said, shaking his hand. "How's the lawdog business these days?"

"Never a dull moment. Here, grab yourself a chair."

Walker was a portly man with muttonchop whiskers and the charm of a born politician. His suits were expensive, tailored to conceal his paunch, and he always smelled freshly scrubbed. He got Stillman seated and then took a chair behind his monolith of a desk.

"We've got a problem," he said, suddenly serious. "One of those damnedable situations where everything comes up short."

"Don't tell me," Stillman remarked idly. "Your boys hit a dead end, right?"

"Exactly!" Walker whacked his desk with an open palm. "A bank robber with the unlikely sobriquet of Whiskey Joe Jones. He's skipping back and forth along the Outlaw Trail, and that makes him a federal fugitive."

Several years past, peace officers had discovered the existence of an Outlaw Trail. Extending from northern Arizona to the Canadian border, it traversed the western territories, with three principal hideouts along the route. The first stop, located in southeastern Utah, was known as Robbers Roost. Farther north, situated in a desolate corner of Colorado, was the second station, Brown's Hole. The last stop on the Outlaw Trail lay some two hundred miles to the northeast, located in the barrens of upper Wyoming. Known simply as Hole-in-the-Wall, it was considered the most impregnable of all the hideouts.

"According to the grapevine," Walker went on, "Jones decided to lay low at Robbers Roost. You're the only officer who ever got inside Hole-in-the-Wall and got out alive. So that makes you a natural to take a crack at Robbers Roost. Sound interesting?"

"Yeah, it does," Stillman said. "Only one hitch."

"What's that?"

"I accepted an assignment not two hours ago."

"Christ!" Walker threw up his hands in exasperation. "None of my men would stand a chance at Robbers Roost. Couldn't you put off this job for a couple of weeks?"

Stillman shook his head. "I've already taken the man's money. Besides that, it's got dibs over your bank robber. Involves four murders."

"Four!" Walker repeated. "Whereabouts?"

"Tenbow Valley," Stillman said. "Out in the Wind Rivers."

Walker's expression turned solemn. "Why, sure, we heard about that. Some bushwhacker's gone wild the last month or so."

"Any of your boys look into it?"

"Out of our jurisdiction, Jack. Strictly a local matter."

"How about the sheriff?" Stillman asked. "Heard anything on him?"

"That's Fremont County," Walker mused aloud. "Sheriff's name is Lon Hubbard. So far as I know, he's a pretty decent lawman."

"Except when it comes to murder."

"Hell, he's a county sheriff, Jack. What do you expect?"

Stillman frowned, considering. "You ever hear of a man named Carl Richter?"

"Not that I recall."

"How about Frank Devlin?"

"No, can't say as I have."

"Will Sontag?"

Walker bobbed his head. "Big rancher, real thick with the Association. Hard-nosed and hell on wheels. Hates homesteaders worse than the Devil hates holy water."

"So I've been told," Stillman said. "You ever hear of him stepping outside the law?"

"Not a peep," Walker responded. "Probably hanged a few rustlers in his time. But hell's fire, we could indict half the Association on that score."

"Yeah, you're right there."

"Wish I could be of more help, Jack."

"I second the motion."

"You're headed for Tenbow, then?"

"Tomorrow morning."

Stillman climbed to his feet. Walker circled the desk and followed him across the room. At the door he hesitated, staring earnestly at Stillman.

"Do me a favor."

"Anything I can, Tom."

"Find that bastard and get your butt back here. I gotta send somebody to Robbers Roost!"

"You could always go yourself."

"What—?"

Stillman laughed, opening the door and letting himself out. He wouldn't soon forget the perplexed expression on Walker's face. The look was worth the trip uptown.

Stillman took his noonday meal in a café frequented by tradespeople. He was largely indifferent to food except as a source of sustenance. Some people lived to eat, marking their day by the routine of mealtime rituals. He ate to live, stoking himself much as a train locomotive was fed coal. Food was fuel, fancy or plain never entering into consideration.

Afterward, he walked down the street to a grocery store. That morning he had decided to travel overland, by horse. Tenbow lay some two hundred and fifty miles northwest of Cheyenne, roughly seven days on the trail. An alternative was to take the train to Rock Springs and travel from there by stage. But that made his departure, as well as his destination, relatively easy to track. By long-standing habit, whenever he accepted an assignment, he covered his tracks to the greatest extent possible. So he'd decided to make the trip on horseback.

Some people might have thought him overly cautious. Yet he operated on the principle that a client, however trustworthy, would always tell someone that he'd been hired. In that event, other parties would know where he was headed and when he might be expected to arrive. What they wouldn't know was how he planned to get there and in what guise he would arrive. For he never traveled as himself, and by a variety of means he always altered his looks. Whatever the scheme of things, he went into an assignment with an edge on those he'd been hired to investigate. On occasion that slight edge had saved his life.

The grocer knew better than to ask questions. He accepted Stillman's list of provisions without comment or curiosity. The items included a coffeepot, skillet, utensils, and a large canteen. Foodstuffs were limited to salt pork, hardtack, coffee beans, and dried fruit. To the grocer the vittles indicated that Stillman meant to travel light and live off the land. Yet he merely nodded, wisely keeping his thoughts to himself. He agreed to deliver the provisions by late afternoon.

From there, Stillman proceeded to a livery stable near the stockyards. He walked directly to a large stall at the rear of the building. Opening the door, he stepped inside and was greeted by a blood bay gelding with a black mane and tail. The horse was barrel-chested, standing fifteen hands high, and weighed well over a thousand pounds. His hide glistened like dark blood on polished redwood, and though spirited, he exhibited an even disposition. He possessed speed and catlike agility, and plenty of bottom for endurance over a long haul.

The bay nuzzled Stillman, whuffing low sounds deep in his throat. He was a one-man horse, and they had shared the trail many times over the years. After rubbing his muzzle and scratching him behind the ears, Stillman subjected the bay to close inspection. He checked the shoes and the frogs of the hooves, slowly circling the horse as he lifted each leg. At the rear of the stall, where gear was stored on an enclosed rack, he then checked his saddle, saddlebags, and rifle scabbard. At length, satisfied with horse and gear, he emerged from the stall.

The owner of the stable was waiting for him. Edgar Watson was a paunchy, whey-faced man, with an eye for livestock and the soul of a bandit. He bought and sold horses as well as operating the stable, and worked on the premise that not all robbery was conducted at the end of a gun. He nodded pleasantly to Stillman.

"How's your bay look?" he said. "Groom him ever' day, just like you told me."

"Looks fine, Edgar," Stillman allowed. "Give him an extra ration of grain tonight. I'll take him out tomorrow."

"Headed off again, are you?"

Stillman ignored the question. "I need a packhorse that's fit to travel. Got anything decent?"

"Never sold nothin' that wasn't."

Watson led him outside to a large stock pen. Some thirty horses stood munching hay scattered on the ground. Stillman circled the fence, checking conformation and general condition. After several minutes he selected a sorrel with one white stocking. Watson observed that he had a good eye for horseflesh.

The price was double what Stillman expected to pay. They dickered awhile, all in the spirit of who could outwit the other. Finally, Watson named a figure that was within ten dollars of a legal holdup. Stillman agreed and told him to be on the lookout for provisions being delivered to the stable. Watson's eyes turned inquisitive, but he stifled the question. Some things were better left unasked.

On the street again, Stillman turned uptown. A short while later, he entered his office and locked the door. Working quietly, he lifted one end of his desk and muscled it aside. With the tip of a knife he then pried one of the floorboards loose and lifted it out. Beneath the floor was a shallow compartment that served as his personal arsenal. Stored there were a sawed-off shotgun, a saddle carbine, a Winchester '76 .45-100, and a match for the Colt holstered at his side. He pulled the Winchester .45-100 from the compartment.

After replacing the floorboard, he returned the desk to its original position. From the bottom drawer of the desk, which was stacked with cartridge boxes, he took a box of .45-100 shells. He then leaned the Winchester in the corner, beside the file cabinets, with the shells on the floor. For a moment he stood reviewing a mental checklist of things needed for the assignment. Apart from the right clothes, which would be used to complete his disguise, everything seemed in order. Later at the hotel he would select an outfit suitable to the role. He'd already decided on the identity he would assume in Tenbow. That left only one unfinished piece of business.

Her name was Laura Martin.

• • •

The house was located on a street east of the business district. Frilly curtains decorated the windows and the furnishings denoted a certain feminine touch. A savory aroma, thick with the smell of beef and gravy, drifted in from the kitchen.

Stillman was slumped in an overstuffed easy chair. From the parlor, where he sat smoking a cheroot, he could see Laura through the kitchen doorway. She was bustling around the stove, working over a battery of pots and pans. Whenever he left town on an assignment, she always insisted on fixing him a home-cooked meal. An intimate supper made their parting all the more memorable.

Laura was attractive and vibrant, a bundle of energy. Taller than most women, she was dark-haired with startling green eyes and a nicely rounded figure. Her husband, a brakeman with the railroad, had been killed in a train accident three years past. Afterward, to support herself, she had opened a dress shop and millinery. Her business flourished as the town grew, and she was now a woman of independent means. By choice, she was also Jack Stillman's woman.

Their relationship was unusual. For the past year neither of them had kept company with anyone else. Apart from the physical attraction, they shared an emotional attachment that was rare for any couple. Yet they had never spoken of marriage and there were no strings attached to their arrangement. Seemingly they were content with their time together, comfortable with what they had today. Tomorrow would take care of itself.

Laura began carrying steaming dishes from the kitchen. Stillman stubbed out his cheroot and joined her at the candlelit table. A pot roast smothered in gravy was accompanied by mashed potatoes, string beans, and a hot loaf of bread. His indifference to food was a running joke between them. She began loading his plate with generous portions.

"Eat every bite," she said, laughter in her eyes. "You'll need your strength."

Stillman played along. "I'll only be on the trail a week."

"Who's talking about the trail?"

"Sounds like you've got something else in mind."

"Could be," she said with a knowing smile. "We'll discuss it after supper."

Stillman grinned. "Are you gonna start making improper advances again?"

"No, not improper," she said in a husky voice. "Thoroughly indecent."

"Hell," Stillman said, forking a hunk of roast. "Let's eat, then."

She laughed, her eyes like green fire in the candlelight.

FOUR

The sun was a brassy dome in the sky. High overhead a hawk floated on smothered wings, a silent hunter. The slopes of rugged brown mountains, dotted with patches of forest land, drifted off toward the horizon. Far in the distance, quartering southward, the barrens of the Great Divide Basin shimmered under a midday haze.

Stillman nudged his bay gelding onward. With the packhorse on a lead rope, he crossed the rocky bank and forded the Sweetwater River. He was four days out of Cheyenne, on a northwesterly course through rolling, hump-backed mountains. His clothes were covered with trail dust, and sweat-streaked stubble traced his jawline. He squinted at the reflection of sun on water as he rode toward the opposite shoreline.

Beyond lay the Oregon Trail. Discovered by

explorers and mountain men, the trail had served as a wilderness route westward for a generation of pioneers. The overland migration of settlers to Oregon began in earnest in 1841. Shoving off from towns in Missouri, long trains of covered wagons loaded with household goods and farm implements traveled in a northwest direction to Fort Kearny, on the southern bend of the Platte River. By following the south bank of the Platte, the wagons proceeded onward to a frontier outpost, Fort Laramie. From there the route traced the North Platte across Wyoming to the mouth of the Sweetwater.

After fording the river, Stillman skirted the rutted trail. The Sweetwater was a winding mountain stream which gradually ascended in a westerly direction to its headwaters at the foot of South Pass. His immediate destination was South Pass City, another two days along the river. He rode at a steady walk, covering thirty to forty miles between sunrise and sundown. Years of wilderness travel had schooled him in a cardinal rule followed by all plainsmen. He never ran his horses, choosing instead to conserve their strength, watering them often and allowing them to graze morning and night. Should the need to run present itself, he wanted his horses fresh and full of ginger. The precaution was by now ingrained as part of his nature.

An hour or so before sunset he began scouting for a campsite. At a dogleg in the river, he found a spot sheltered by trees with a swath of grass along the shoreline. He unsaddled the bay and removed the packs, snugly wrapped in canvas, from the sorrel. Then he hobbled the horses, preventing them from moving far from camp, and turned them loose to graze. He next gathered an armload of wood from beneath the trees and built a fire within a small circle of rocks. By the time he was ready to eat, the fire would have burnt down to coals suitable for cooking.

From one of the packs he removed a bundle of line wound around a stake, with several fishhooks attached. He unwound the line, jabbed the stake into the bank, and tied a large rock to the opposite end. Unwrapping the salt pork, he used his belt knife to trim off small chunks, which were baited onto the fish hooks. Finished, he stood and heaved the rock into the river, stretching a twenty-foot line between the bank and deep water. The rig was not foolproof, but it worked more often than not. He seldom went without one or more trout for supper.

Stillman rarely let a day pass without testing his gun hand. Even in Cheyenne he usually found time to get out of town and burn some powder. Experience had taught him that lawmen who took their skill for granted too often put their lives at risk. A gunfight was a thing of seconds, generally with no forewarning and no time for thought. Habit and training, fashioned into instinctive reaction, invariably separated the quick from the dead. His business was hunting men, hardly a job to be taken lightly. He kept himself honed to a fine edge.

The Winchester slipped easily from his saddle scabbard. Looking downriver, he selected a dead branch on a tree a hundred yards away. He shouldered the rifle, working the lever, and sighted on the base of the branch. Wood chips flew as he fired and the branch wobbled under the impact. He jacked a fresh shell into the chamber and the sharp crack of the .45-100 echoed along the river. The dead branch split, dangling loosely a moment, and dropped to the ground. He loaded two fresh cartridges into the rifle, then returned it to the scabbard.

Some ten yards downriver he selected a tree roughly the breadth of a man. Stooping down, he gathered a rock off the ground and tossed it downstream. He watched, eyes fastened on the rock, until it splashed in the water. His hand moved in a blur, thumbing the hammer on the Colt as he extended it at shoulder level. He fired five times, with scarcely a heartbeat between shots. Centered on the tree was a cluster of neat holes, all within a handspan of one another. He finished the drill by quickly ejecting the spent shells and inserting fresh loads. Contrary to popular notions, safety dictated that a six-gun be carried with the hammer resting on an empty chamber. He snapped the loading gate closed and holstered the Colt.

The campfire was slowly turning to a bed of cherry-hot coals. He walked to the riverbank and began hauling in the fish line. When he got it on shore, three fat trout flopped about on hooks. In short order he dressed the trout and rinsed them off at the edge of the river. After crushing coffee beans inside a cloth, he filled the coffeepot and set it on rocks beside the coals. Strips of salt pork were used to grease the skillet, and before long the trout were simmering to a golden brown. He settled back to await supper.

Westward, the sun dipped toward the peaks of distant mountains. Stillman suddenly tensed, alerted by the sound of hooves on rock not far downstream. He rose to his feet, moving clear of the fire as he grabbed the Winchester. Out of the corner of his eye he saw the horses stop grazing and stare toward the river. He positioned himself beside a tree, thumb hooked over the hammer of the Winchester. The sound of hoofbeats drew closer.

Several moments passed before two horsemen emerged from the tree line. One was large and beefy, with close-set eyes and shaggy hair. The other was a man of medium build, somewhat younger, a brace of pistols holstered on his gun belt. Their clothes were rough and grimy, their faces streaked with trail dust. They reined to a halt at the edge of the clearing.

"Hello, the camp," the older man called out. "Anybody around?"

Stillman stepped from the shade of the tree. "Afternoon, gents."

The men appeared startled by his sudden appearance. Their eyes fixed on the Winchester and a moment passed in silence. The big one smiled, jerking his thumb downriver.

"We heard shooting a ways back. Thought mebbe somebody was in trouble."

"No trouble," Stillman said. "Just a little target practice."

The big one apparently did the talking for both men. "Mind if we step down, neighbor? Looks like you got yourself a bait of fish."

Stillman watched as they dismounted. "I only caught enough for supper," he said. "You boys are welcome to use my line, though."

The younger one finally spoke. "Stingy bastard, ain't you?" he said roughly. "Whyn't you break out some of the grub in them packs?"

"Hold it!" Stillman ordered as the older one

moved toward the opposite side of the fire. "I just changed my mind. You boys better ride on."

"Like hell," the younger one grunted. "We're gonna have a look in them packs."

The words were meant to distract Stillman. As the younger one started toward the packs, the older man clawed at his holstered pistol. Stillman shot him before he cleared leather and he tumbled backward down the riverbank. Dropping to the ground, Stillman took cover at the base of the tree, working the Winchester lever as a slug peeled bark above his head. He fired and a red splotch blossomed on the younger man's shirtfront. His legs buckled and the pistol slipped from his hand. He slumped to the ground.

Stillman stood, levering a fresh load into the Winchester. Downriver, the men's spooked horses went crashing through the trees. He circled the bodies, checking for any sign of life, and kicked their guns aside. Just as he expected, they were both dead. The .45-100 had dusted them front and back.

There was no aftereffect, no remorse on Stillman's part. The men had started the fight and he figured they'd got what they deserved. Yet a cold sensation settled deep in the pit of his stomach. He wondered whether they had trailed him from Cheyenne. Were they hired guns, working for whoever was behind the

Tenbow killings? Hired by someone who was aware of his assignment and meant to stop him before he got started? Or were they merely robbers, stumbling upon what looked to be an easy mark?

Hard questions but no easy answers. He moved to the fire and set the skillet aside. The trout were burned black and probably tasteless as dry grass. Worse, he had two dead men as company for supper.

All in all, it had been a helluva day.

South Pass City was a ghost town. The streets were overgrown with weeds and brush, and the buildings stood abandoned. Doors hung ajar, roofs were rotted and caved in, and hardly a window was left unbroken. Nothing human lived there any longer.

Stillman reined to a halt outside town. Two days had passed since the shooting, and his appearance was by now even more grungy. He sat staring down the main street at the desolate town and its ramshackle buildings. He remembered a time, not six years past, when he'd come here as a deputy U.S. marshal. The outlaw he'd been chasing had been taken alive in a dance hall filled with miners and fancy women. South Pass City in those days had been a riproaring boomtown.

The origin of the town's name stemmed

from South Pass itself. Situated on the Continental Divide in the Central Rockies, the pass was fabled as the gateway to Oregon. Early travelers were often unaware that they had crossed the great divide, once a barrier to the Far West. To the north of the pass lay the Wind River range, and the Antelope Hills bordered it on the south. But the pass itself was actually a saddle between mountain ranges, a broad plain twenty miles wide, which rose imperceptibly from a lowland basin to a height of nearly eight thousand feet. Twelve miles beyond, travelers saw streams flowing westward and realized they had crossed the Continental Divide.

From there the Oregon Trail crossed southwest through Green River valley to Fort Bridges. The rutted track then turned northwest through Idaho, to Fort Hall on the Snake River. Farther on, across the Blue Mountains, lay the Columbia and the Promised Land, Oregon. The journey of nearly two thousand miles took four to six months, and left the landscape littered with lonely graves and abandoned wagons. Between 1841 and 1860, upward of 300,000 settlers pushed westward across the Oregon Trail.

Some eighty miles southwest of South Pass, the town of Rock Springs began as a waystation on the Overland Stage route. Later, the Union Pacific chose to lay track along the same route because of the area's abundant coal deposits, which fueled the locomotives. In 1867, gold was discovered within the hard-rock lode twelve miles north of South Pass, and the rush was on. By 1871, South Pass City was a wild and woolly boomtown, boasting a population of 4,000 people. That same year the Union Pacific ran a spur line north, across the Continental Divide, with end-of-track at the mining camp.

Stillman recalled that the boom had lasted roughly four years. Early in 1875, the lode played out and the exodus began in earnest. By the end of that year South Pass City was deserted, the saloons and dance halls stilled forever. Today, as he stared along the main street, the town lay in ruins, a shabby remnant of its glory days. Towns, like men, sometimes lived and died in a short but spectacular burst of fame. He turned from the sight, oddly saddened by the memory of what once had been.

That night he camped along a creek on the outskirts of town. Since the shooting he'd grown increasingly vigilant, halting at regular intervals to watch his back-trail. By now, if the dead men were in fact hired guns, their boss would know that the plan had failed. All the more disturbing, whoever was responsible would know that he was drawing ever closer to Tenbow. Other hired guns might have been sent to waylay him along the remote trail into the Wind Rivers. One man traveling alone could be ambushed with great ease in the wilderness.

So easy, in fact, that he halfway doubted his own suspicions. A hundred times in the past two days he'd replayed in his head the details of the shooting. Suppose the dead men had been set on his trail, ordered to kill him. Were that the case, why had they ridden boldly into his camp? Why hadn't they laid an ambush instead at some isolated spot? Why risk a head-to-head encounter, knowing that he was no slouch with a gun? Something was out of kilter about the whole affair, the sloppy way they'd picked a fight. Of course, nothing decreed that hired guns had to be mental giants. Some men were born dumb and died dumb.

Yet, for all the unanswered questions, he couldn't discount the likelihood that he was a target. From everything Carl Richter had told him, the man behind the Tenbow killings was shrewd as well as ruthless. Four men killed without a single clue indicated someone capable of devious, farsighted planning. Such a man would be equally capable of orchestrating the death of a private detective who traveled alone. All the more so when Carl Richter, despite his promise of silence, had probably told someone, maybe several people, about his trip to Cheyenne. But even then something still didn't ring true. The dead men were just too reckless, too foolhardy. Looking back, they seemed to him a couple of down-at-the-heels drifters. Dimdots impersonating authentic toughnuts.

On the creek, setting up camp, he decided the whole thing was an imponderable. Lots of questions, lots of maybes, but few facts and no answers. He hobbled the horses and turned them out to graze. Then, after building a fire, he dressed a rabbit he'd shot outside town. When the fire burned down, he would spit the rabbit and roast it over the coals. He reminded himself that tomorrow morning he had to shave. A week's growth of beard covered his face.

Tonight, as he had for the past two nights, he planned to let the fire die out. High in the mountains, a chill settled over the land even during the summer. A fire was a comforting thing, pushing back the darkness and providing warmth. But a fire left him exposed and vulnerable, an easy kill for anyone who discovered his camp. Darkness was now his ally, especially if there were men from Tenbow sent to hunt him down. So tonight he'd roll up in his bedroll and sleep light. With the Colt near at hand.

Once the rabbit was spitted, his thoughts turned to tomorrow. Tenbow was roughly thirty miles to the north, an easy day's ride. He planned to arrive there as someone other than himself, a stranger with a reason for traveling distant mountains. Thinking about it now, he unfastened the straps on one of the packs. From inside he withdrew a neatly folded broadcloth coat, somber black and finely tailored. He then removed a pair of Nankeen trousers, a white shirt, and a four-in-hand tie. The next item, wrapped in satin cloth, was a ruby stickpin only slightly smaller than a rifle slug.

The key to his disguise was in a leather pouch, the interior padded with fleecy wool. Opening it, he removed what appeared to be a small sleeve of gold, half the size of a thumbnail. The sleeve was thin and intricately crafted, with tiny rounded clips on the reverse side. Last year Stillman had proposed the idea to a dentist, who worked on the project with the skill of an artisan. He now slipped the sleeve onto the lower edge of his right front tooth and pushed upward. The sleeve covered the front and bottom of the tooth, and the clips held it securely in place from the rear. The visual effect was that of a gold tooth.

Stillman used the device much as a magician employs misdirection. Show the crowd one thing, distract their attention, and perform magic with the other hand. In Stillman's variation, whenever he smiled, even when he talked, other people's eyes were drawn to the sparkle of the tooth. Their focus was on the gleam of gold rather than the man, and the deception worked better than he'd ever imagined. Over the past year he had used it on two assignments, and in each instance the gold tooth had embellished his overall disguise. He was confident that it would serve equally well in Tenbow.

Later that night, he lay wrapped in his bedroll. The fire was extinguished and the horses were hitched to a nearby tree. There was no moon, and the indigo sky was sprinkled with stars. Not yet able to sleep, he stared at the heavens, locating the North Star, the outer star on the handle of the Little Dipper. At sunrise, he would ride north into the vastness of the Wind River mountains. Waiting there were men who would kill him, given the slightest opportunity. The thought brought a smile, a renewed sense of anticipation. He wanted to hurry the night, awaken to a crisp dawn. Press ahead to Tenbow.

Where the hunt would begin.

FIVE

Wild honeysuckle belled softly in a faint breeze, bright petals aflame in the afternoon sun. Tufted redbirds flitted among wolfberry bushes on the slopes while overhead bluebirds swept from the sky in flat, shallow dives. Below, in the willows along the river, redwings scolded and chirred, darting scarlet flashes against the leafy green.

Stillman rode north through Tenbow Valley. The trail snaked and turned, angling off in a northeasterly direction. To the west, the Wind River mountains thrust awesomely skyward, massive links in the Continental Divide. The snowcapped peaks, towering twelve thousand feet or more, stood in bold silhouette against cottony clouds. The sheer grandeur left a solitary rider somehow humbled, curiously diminished.

Since sunrise, the trail had led Stillman ever

deeper into the remote valley. Eastward, the spires of the Wind Rivers dropped off sharply, forming a lower range some five thousand feet in elevation. Flowing from the higher peaks were the Popo Agie River and its many forks. These streams crossed through Tenbow Valley, forming a latticework of watered meadowlands and forested canyons. The valley itself stretched northwestward for a distance of some eighty miles.

Scattered throughout the valley were ranches and homesteads. From his meeting with Carl Richter, Stillman knew that the cattlemen and farmers maintained an uneasy truce. While the Indian wars still raged, the valley had belonged to pioneer cattlemen, pushing ever deeper into tribal lands. Open range was an unwritten law, and cattlemen claimed vast sections of grazeland without legal title. At one time, four or five cattle barons had ruled the whole of Tenbow Valley.

The Homestead Act, passed by Congress in 1862, altered a way of life for western cattlemen. The bill enabled settlers to homestead any surveyed but unclaimed tract of public land. The settlers were allowed a quarter-section, or 160 acres, and title was granted after five years. The floodtide westward increased manyfold following the army's campaign against the great Sioux and Cheyenne alliance.

Within the past two years, homesteaders had settled throughout the breadth of Tenbow Valley. For cattlemen, the days of open range were ended forever.

Yet there was prosperity even in the midst of change. From his time as a marshal, Stillman recalled that the Wind River Reservation was located only five miles north of Tenbow. A treaty with the Shoshoni tribe in 1868 had granted them an enormous block of land north and south of the Wind River. During the Indian wars the Shoshoni chose to follow their great peace leader, Chief Washaki. The fighting raged all around them, but the Shoshoni refused to join in the bloodshed. The people and their lands were spared the destruction that befell other tribes.

The Arapho were not so fortunate. Along with the Sioux and the Cheyenne, they took part in Custer's defeat at the battle of Little Big Horn. Following the battle, the Arapaho remained allied with Crazy Horse until his surrender to the army in 1877. Soon afterward, what remained of the Northern Arapaho, nine hundred destitute men, women, and children, were settled on the Wind River Reservation. The Shoshoni gave ground, confined to the western half of the reservation, and the Arapaho occupied the eastern half. There the two tribes, one peaceful and the other conquered, lived in squalid harmony.

The cattlemen of Tenbow Valley prospered most from the arrangement. The reservation tribes were dependent upon the government for virtually every aspect of their subsistence. Food and clothing were distributed throughout the year, all acquired by agency contract. Cows supplied by nearby ranchers provided beef, which became a staple for Indians no longer able to hunt for their meat. Other foodstuffs and clothing were supplied by local merchants, who profited handsomely from goods freighted overland by wagon. Open range had disappeared with the settlers, and the larger cattlemen still resented their invasion of the valley. But the proximity of the reservation insured that everyone benefited from a stable economy.

Stillman rode into Tenbow shortly before sunset. The town consisted of a main street running north and south, with houses scattered along narrow side streets. There were two banks, a newspaper, stores of various descriptions, and a single hotel. The county courthouse was located at the north end of town, across from a church and the schoolhouse. All the buildings were constructed of wood, but there was something substantial about the mountain community. The usual saloons and gaming dens detracted not at all from the air of permanence. Everything looked built to last.

On the south edge of town Stillman found a livery stable. After paying for stalls, he collected his saddlebags and rifle and walked uptown. Supper time was quickly approaching and stores along the street were closing for the night. At the hotel, which was a two-story affair with a fresh coat of whitewash, he turned into the lobby. A balding room clerk nodded as he halted before the desk.

"Evening," Stillman said. "I'd like the best room in the house."

The clerk eyed his ruby stickpin and gold tooth. "Be stayin' long, Mr.—?"

"Drummond," Stillman informed him. "Duke Drummond. Nice little town you've got here."

"We sorta like it ourselves."

"I'll pay you a week in advance. We'll see how things go after that."

"Yessir, Mr. Drummond! Pleased to have you as a guest."

Duke Drummond's profession was never in question. The flashy clothes, abetted by the gold tooth, identified him in the clerk's mind as an itinerant gambler. Such men traveled the West, drifting from town to town, plying their trade. Tenbow was somewhat off the beaten path, but it was a prosperous community. Professional gamblers occasionally stopped off to try their luck with local high rollers.

Stillman carried his belongings to a room on the second floor. He was confident that word of his arrival would spread through town within the hour. The room clerk looked to be a talker, and passing gamblers were always news. After washing up, he went back downstairs. He asked directions to a good café as well as the best saloon in town. The clerk pointed him up the street.

The Bon Ton Café proved to be a popular establishment. Quickly filling with the suppertime crowd, there was a lull in conversation as Stillman entered and took a table near the door. The townspeople subjected him to a brief inspection, then the buzz of conversation slowly resumed. The evening special was beef stew, soda biscuits, and dried apple pie. The food was plain but tasty, particularly after seven days on the trail. He took his time, lingering over a second cup of coffee. The room was half empty when he rose to leave.

Outside, he crossed the street and entered the Tivoli Saloon. A long bar backed by a large mirror occupied one side of the room. Opposite the bar was a faro layout and twenty-one table, the latter manned by a house dealer. Toward the rear were three tables, the center one covered with green felt. For a small town, he thought it looked promising.

Several men were standing at the bar and a

lone player sat before the twenty-one dealer.
Stillman took a spot at the end of the counter,
lighting a cheroot. The barkeep, a heavyset
man with sagging jowls, ambled over. He nodded without expression.

"What's your pleasure?"

"Whiskey," Stillman said. "And some information."

"Lemme guess," the barkeep observed.
"You're a gamblin' man looking for a game."

"You the owner?"

"Only when we turn a profit."

Stillman grinned, the gold tooth gleaming
brightly. "I'm Duke Drummond," he said.
"Poker's my game and I deal honest cards."

"You'd damn well better," the barkeep said.
"Last tinhorn through here barely got out alive."

"How're you fixed for men with sporting
blood?"

"You set up shop and they'll be around.
Course, I'll expect a little something for steerin'
them in your direction."

"Sounds fair to me."

Stillman walked to the felt-covered table. He
took a chair and pulled a deck of cards from his
coat pocket. The cheroot wedged in the corner
of his mouth, he began dealing solitaire. There
were two bar girls at the end of the counter, and
one of them brought his whisky. She set the
glass beside him on the table.

"Welcome to the Tivoli," she said smiling. "The boss says the first one's on the house."

"Tell him I'm obliged."

She laughed. "Nothing's free in this joint. He'll get his—if you win."

"Well, now, I surely don't aim to lose!"

Stillman watched as she turned away. Her ruffled dress was knee-length and peek-a-boo at the top. Her figure was slim but rounded and her legs were nicely turned. Looking past her, he saw the barkeep talking to two men who had just entered. One was short and stocky, and wore a fashionably tailored suit. The other was a tall, hulking man with blunt features and hard eyes. The telltale bulge of a pistol was visible beneath his coat.

The short man glanced toward the poker table, then nodded to the barkeep. He turned, motioning to his companion, and walked along the bar. As they approached, Stillman noted the taller one's brutish appearance, like a pugilist in search of a fight. They halted before the table and the shorter one gave him a foxy look.

"Hear you play poker," he said. "I'm partial to the game myself."

"Drag up a chair," Stillman said, waving his cheroot. "Maybe we can get a game started."

"Wouldn't surprise me in the least."

The shorter one seated himself across the table. As though on cue, the taller man took a position directly behind his chair. From all appearances, one played while the other stood guard. The bar girl brought a fresh round of drinks and a sealed deck of cards. Stillman popped the seal with his thumbnail and began shuffling.

"Duke Drummond's the name," he said. "Only fair to tell you, playing poker is my trade."

"Pleased to make your acquaintance, Mr. Drummond. I'm Frank Devlin."

There was no introduction of the taller one. But Stillman immediately placed the name of the man seated opposite him. Frank Devlin was the land speculator, one of the two men he'd been hired to investigate. He thought it a good omen, almost a stroke of luck.

Poker often revealed much about a man.

The table was bathed in the cider glow of an overhead lamp. There were six players, including Stillman and Devlin. One of the others, a notions drummer, was dealing draw poker. No one spoke as cards whisked around the table.

All of them had agreed that this would be the last hand. They had been playing for almost six hours, and it was well after midnight. Tenbow locked up early; the last customer had departed some time ago. Behind the counter, the barkeep and one of the girls were washing glasses. The girl waiting on the table stood watching the game.

Stillman was ahead by more than two hundred dollars. He'd been the steady winner, drawing unbeatable hands for a good part of the night. One by one, the other players had taken a chair in the game. Aside from the drummer, there was a hardware store owner, the stage company manager, and a lawyer. By mutual agreement the betting limit was ten dollars, check and raise allowed.

Western rules still prevailed in the mountains. Some Eastern casinos had revised the traditional rules of poker to create more enticing odds for high rollers. Introduced into the game were straights, flushes, and the most elusive of all combinations, the straight flush. The highest hand back east was now a royal flush, ten through ace in the same suit.

Poker in the West was still played by the original rules. Whether draw or stud poker, there were two unbeatable hands. The first was four aces, drawn by most players only once or twice in a lifetime. The other was four kings with an ace, which precluded anyone holding four aces. Seasoned players looked upon it as a minor miracle or the work of a skilled cardsharp. Four kings in combination with an ace surmounted almost incalculable odds.

As the last hand was dealt, Stillman found

himself holding three kings with a trey and a nine. The correct play would have been to discard the trey and nine, hoping to catch the fourth king on the draw. Or perhaps a matched pair to round out a full house. But he was wary of winning too heavily his first night in town. The cooperation of the townspeople was essential to his investigation, and he wanted no ill feelings. He decided to lose in a flashy manner.

Devlin was under the gun, seated next to the dealer, and he opened for ten dollars. The lawyer called the bet and the hardware man raised it five. Stillman pretended to study his cards, then raised it another five. The stage-line manager grunted something under his breath and folded his hand. The drummer folded as well, and Devlin grinned, toying a moment with his stack of gold coins. He took the last raise for ten dollars.

Stillman was a skilled poker player. Over the years he had schooled himself in the game, learning the tricks of cardsharps as well as the odds on any hand. At the same time he had a natural gift for reading men, discerning what lay beneath the surface. Several times tonight he'd caught Devlin bluffing, trying to buy a hand. He thought the land speculator's last raise was yet another bluff.

After everyone had called, the dealer announced, "Cards to the players." Devlin discarded two, indicating he held three of a kind. The lawyer frowned, asking for three cards, and the hardware man took two. Stillman split his three kings, discarding a king and a nine. On the draw, he caught an ace and the case king. Studying the cards, he realized that he might yet have the best hand. Three kings with an ace kicker meant that no one could be holding four aces. And he seriously doubted that the hardware man had improved his three of a kind.

Devlin, as the original opener, bet the limit. The lawyer folded and the hardware man merely called. Stillman raised ten dollars, and Devlin bumped it another ten. The hardware store owner deliberated a moment, then called both raises. Stillman refused the final raise, shoving ten dollars into the pot. Had he raised, he would have been required to show his hand first. He thought he had both men beat and he wanted to see their cards. Only then could he lose in a believable fashion.

True to form, Devlin had tried to run a bluff. As the last raiser, he turned over his cards, revealing a pair of tens. The hardware man slowly spread his hand, fanning three queens. Stillman shook his head, staring at the queens, and tossed his cards on the deadwood. By acknowledging the queens as the winner, he was not obligated to show his hand. The hardware store owner laughed and raked in the pot. Devlin gave Stillman a strange look, then shrugged. The other players began pocketing their money.

The game over, the men drifted toward the door. Devlin was the last to leave, trailed by his hard-eyed companion. Stillman remained seated at the table, ostensibly counting his winnings. But his gaze was on Devlin, and he wondered what he'd learned tonight. A couple of times between hands, the players had spoken of the mysterious killings. Acting the newcomer, Stillman had drawn them out, hoping to gather further information. Nothing of consequence was revealed about the killings, yet he'd been intrigued by a seeming oddity. Frank Devlin hadn't once joined in the conversation, or voiced an opinion on the murders. His silence was something to think about.

"How'd you do?"

Stillman looked up as the bar girl took a chair at the table. Underneath the warpaint she was an attractive woman, somewhere in her late twenties. Her hair was auburn and her eyes held a certain bawdy wisdom. He nodded indifferently to her question.

"Won enough to tide me over."

"Come off it!" she said with a knowing smile. "You ditched that last hand, didn't you? You had them beat."

"What makes you think that?"

"Oh, just a hunch. Don't stiff 'em too hard and they'll keep coming back to your table. Am I right?"

Stillman chuckled. "You ought to take up gamblin'."

"Sweetie, I've been a gambler all my life. How else do you think I got stuck in this one-horse town?"

"What's your name?"

"Jennie Blake," she said. "And your moniker's Duke Drummond. The boss told me."

"I'm curious about something." Stillman waited until she nodded. "That Devlin fellow and his sidekick that never talks? What's the story on them?"

"Devlin's harmless," she said. "Lots of money and pretty proud of himself. But don't mess with his watchdog."

"The bruiser?"

"Yeah, his name's Monty Johnson. Supposed to be fast with a gun and and faster with his fists. Scares the hell outta me."

Stillman looked puzzled. "Why would Devlin need a watchdog?"

"Pure greed," she said quickly. "Him and a rancher named Sontag keep butting heads. They're both trying to buy up the valley—and Devlin pays better."

"Has Sontag threatened him?"

"I guess so," she said. "Anyway, that's why everybody figures he's got Johnson on the payroll."

Stillman considered a moment. There was antagonism between Devlin and Will Sontag, the other suspect in the case. But their personal hard feeling had no apparent connection to the murders. Unless, of course, there was something he hadn't yet uncovered.

"I was thinking," Jennie said in a low voice. "I've got my own room upstairs. Why don't you come up for a drink?"

When Stillman hesitated, she rushed on: "I could give you the lowdown on everybody who's anybody in town. We might even team up, hook 'em into your game."

"Sounds like my kind of proposition."

Stillman followed her toward a stairwell at the rear of the room. Saloon girls often overheard choice gossip, and he thought she might know something worth hearing. If not, then he could leave after a drink. Or stay, depending on how things went.

Jennie led him up the stairs, her pulse quickening with each step. She'd waited a long time for a change in luck, and tonight was the night. Her every instinct told her it would work.

Duke Drummond was her ticket out of Tenbow!

SIX

Faint light from a pale sickle moon streamed through the window. Stillman lay awake in his darkened hotel room, staring at the ceiling. Hands locked behind his head, he slowly reviewed the past two days. All of it struck him as separating the wheat from the chaff.

Experience had taught him the tricks of subtle interrogation. For two days now he had passed himself off as the amiable gambler. He'd talked at length with the desk clerk, who also happened to own the hotel. At the café, where he took all his meals, he had fallen into conversation with other customers. Earlier tonight he'd pumped a couple of townsmen at the Tivoli bar. Later, during the poker game, he had again prompted speculative discussion about the killings. Everything he'd heard was a mixture of confusion and fear.

Frank Devlin, everyone agreed, was sympa-

thetic to the common people, farmers and
small ranchers. Moreover, he was a fair man,
and generous, paying top price for land. After
every killing, he had called on the widow, offering condolences and paying cash on the spot
for a quitclaim deed. To hear him tell it, there
were great times ahead in Tenbow Valley, and
he meant to make his fortune buying and selling to settlers. Yet under tactful questioning, a
curious fact had emerged from any conversation about Devlin. He'd bought several pieces
of land, including the four spreads from the
widows of slain men. But he had yet to sell the
first piece of land. He seemed content to buy
and hold.

The talk about Will Sontag was more to the
point. Everyone agreed that the former cattle
baron was a hard man, stubborn and cantan-
kerous and stiff-necked with pride. He had no
family apart from his wife and he apparently
wanted no friends. He considered settlers a
pestilence on the land and treated other cattlemen with a mild form of contempt. The end of
open range had reduced his spread by more
than half, and along with it, the size of his
herd. But he was nonetheless well-off, a tight-
fisted skinflint who still had his first nickel. Determined to rebuild his cattle empire, he'd tried
and failed to outbid Devlin on various parcels
of land. Word had it that he was furious at be-

ing done out by a johnny-come-lately. He still thought of Tenbow Valley as his own private stomping grounds.

The story was the same everywhere. Frank Devlin was considered a decent man with a taste for land speculation. Will Sontag was a miserly bastard whose grand obsession was to regain control of the valley. Yet neither of them, according to conventional wisdom, were thought to have any part in the killings. For all that, fear was nonetheless pervasive among the townspeople as well as the outlying farmers and ranchers. There was widespread belief that the murders were intended to drive people from their land. No one could hazard a guess as to the reason, and it seemed somehow too sinister to fathom. But there was solid accord on the most frightening aspect of the whole business. No one thought the killings had yet ended.

Tonight, after the poker game, Stillman had declined Jennie's invitation. Having spent last night in her room, he knew there was nothing left for her to tell. Eager to please, she had related every tidbit of gossip she'd ever heard. But none of it had provided even a vague hint as to who was behind the killings. Like the townspeople, everything she knew was hardly worth the listening. So he'd disappointed her, even though she was pleasant company. Another night in her room would lead nowhere, and he had returned instead to the hotel. He needed time to think things through.

Barely an hour had passed while he lay staring at the ceiling. But now, having examined the case from every angle, he rolled out of bed and walked to the window. The town was dark beneath pale moonlight, the streets empty. He stood there a long while, reluctant to admit a hard truth. For all his nosing around, he'd drawn a blank in Tenbow. The investigation was at a stalemate.

Nothing he'd uncovered incriminated Frank Devlin. The land speculator had a motive for the murders, as indicated by his rush to buy the property of those slain. But no one had witnessed the killings, and there was no physical evidence that established a direct link to Devlin. Nor was there any way to verify his whereabouts on the days the killings took place. The same thought applied to his hard-eyed watchdog, Monty Johnson. Too much time had passed since the murders.

Stillman slowly turned his attention to Will Sontag. By all accounts, the rancher was tough and ruthless. There was also motive: an obsession to regain control of the valley, buttressed by open animosity toward newcomers. All that, of course, was rumor and speculation, voiced by people who held the rancher in low regard.

More often than not, however, there was some element of truth in such widespread agreement. Yet to confirm allegations about the cattleman required something more than talking to townspeople. Will Sontag had to be investigated on his own ground.

The decision made, Stillman turned his attention to details. The first order of business was to depart Tenbow without arousing suspicion. His hotel room was paid for a week, so that presented no problem. He could leave before daylight with little fear of being spotted. People might wonder where he'd gone, but some reasonable explanation could be offered when he returned. The critical step was reclaiming his bay gelding from the livery stable. For he planned to depart Tenbow as someone other than Duke Drummond. A new disguise, another man entirely.

From his saddlebags he removed a pair of faded trousers and a work shirt. He changed clothes and strapped the holstered Colt around his waist. His gambler's outfit, including the ruby stickpin, was left hanging on wall pegs. With his rifle and saddlebags he stepped into the hall and locked the door. Quietly he made his way down the stairs and paused to inspect the lobby. The lamps were turned low and there was no one behind the room clerk's desk. A clock on the wall indicated the time was just shy of three in the morning. He crossed the lobby and eased the door open. The street was empty.

A few minutes later, he slipped through he door of the livery stable. As he approached the stalls, he began talking softly, calming the bay. The packhorse, which he would leave behind, scarcely glanced in his direction. Working quickly, he took a battered leather vest, trail boots, and a rough jacket from one of the canvas packs. Wrapped in the jacket were a pair of spurs with large, spiked rowels. He shrugged into the vest and jacket, changed boots, and strapped on the spurs. After saddling the bay, he lashed his saddlebags and bedroll behind the cantle. The rifle was jammed into its saddle scabbard.

Opening the stall door, he led the bay to the front of the stable. There he paused and slipped under the office door a note he'd written at the hotel. The message was signed Duke Drummond and explained that he would be out of town for a few days. Outside, he gingerly closed the stable door and stepped into the saddle. He rode north from Tenbow.

A short distance along the road he remembered the gold tooth. He reined to a halt, removed the tooth, and stowed it deep in his saddlebags. The last vestige of the gambling man disappeared with the tooth. He now assumed another guise.

His name was Cliff Jordan.

The Lazy S was situated on the North Fork of the Popo Agie. Some ten miles northwest of Tenbow, the ranch was surrounded by mountains and woodlands. The tributary flowed through a section of the valley that was relatively flat and lush with graze. Far to the west, the Wind Rivers stood in bold relief against an azure sky.

Headquarters for the Lazy S was located along a gentle bend in the river. The main house, a sprawling affair constructed of logs, dominated the compound. The bunkhouse and cook shack were positioned off to one side, with a large corral and several outbuildings nearby. There was a sense of isolation and mountain splendor about the site.

Stillman rode into the compound at sunrise. From stories he'd heard, he knew that Will Sontag had selected the headquarters site some fifteen years ago. Though he'd made friends with the Shoshoni, he'd had to withstand raids from hostile tribes as he slowly carved a ranch from the wilderness. But now, with an end to open range, his spread was a mere shadow of the past. These days the Lazy S ran less than five thousand head of cattle.

A gang of cowhands was gathered outside the corral. With breakfast finished and their horses saddled, they stood smoking roll-your-owns, ready for the day's work. They watched in silence as Stillman reined to a halt, eyeing the rider as well as the lines of his bay gelding. By unwritten custom a stranger never dismounted until invited to step down. He nodded to the silent faces.

"Mornin'," he said. "The foreman around?"

"Nope," one of the hands replied. "We ain't got a foreman no more."

"Who's in charge?"

"The boss," the hand informed him. "Mr. Sontag."

"Where would I find him?"

"Just over your right shoulder."

Stillman turned in the saddle. He saw a beefy man with sullen features walking down from the main house. He placed Sontag's age on the sundown side of forty. On the porch, he spotted a woman several years younger, watching them. He recalled that Sontag had a wife but no children. When Sontag stopped near the corral, he knuckled the brim of his hat.

"Mornin', Mr. Sontag," he said, adopting the speech pattern of men who worked livestock. "I come by lookin' to hire out."

"Got all the hands I need," Sontag said

shortly. "See the cook if you want some breakfast."

"Don't punch cows," Stillman said. "I break horses."

Throughout the spring and summer, bronc busters drifted across the West. They hired on with ranches to break horses, seldom expecting steady work. Some worked by the day, others contracted at a fixed rate for each horse.

Sontag looked him over. "What's your name?"

"Cliff Jordan."

"How do I know you can do the job?"

"Simple," Stillman said, grinning. "Gimme a critter nobody's rode."

"Slim," Sontag said to one of the hands, "go get that grizzle bear that calls hisself a horse." He nodded to Stillman. "You stick on this one and mebbe we'll talk."

Shortly a rangy buckskin gelding had been lassoed from horses milling around the corral. The buckskin fought the rope, kicking and snorting as Slim moved him toward the gate. Some of the other hands jumped to assist, and they gradually worked the bronc into a breaking pen near the main corral. Slim snubbed him up short to a fence post.

Stillman entered the breaking pen. He took a hack-amore off the top rail, talking softly all the

while, and slipped it over the buckskin's head.
Then he used a saddle blanket to blindfold the
horse, and with his other hand he tossed a saddle into place. The buckskin flinched but stood
still, calmed by the blindfold. With his free
hand Stillman reached under and caught the
cinch ring. Before the horse could react, he
stepped to the side, threaded the latigo, and
jerked the cinch tight. The buckskin started to
rear back, but he slipped the noose from
around its neck and grabbed the reins. He
stepped into the saddle.

The buckskin exploded at both ends. All
four hooves left the ground as the horse bowed
its back and in the next instant stretched outward in a bone-jarring snap. Then it swapped
ends in midair and sunfished across the corral
in a series of bounding, catlike leaps. Stillman
was all over the animal, bouncing from one
side to the other, never twice in the same spot.
Veering away from the fence, the bronc
whirled and kicked, slamming him front to
rear in the saddle. His hat went spinning skyward in a lazy arc.

Stillman lifted his boots high, raked hard
across the shoulders with his spurs. The spiked
rowels whirred like a buzz saw and the buckskin roared a great squeal of outrage. Leaping
straight upward in the air, the bronc swallowed
its head and humped its back. A moment later it

hit on all four hooves with a jolt that shook the earth. Then the horse went berserk, erupting in a beeline toward the corral fence. Stillman swung out of the saddle at the exact instant the buckskin collided with the cross timbers.

Staggered, the bronc buckled at the knees and fell back on its rump. For several moments it sat there, head wobbling like a woozy drunk. Stillman stepped back into the saddle as the horse regained its legs, rammed his spurs into the flanks. There was less rage this time, ending in a series of stiff-legged crowhops that lacked power. Stillman hauled back on the hack-amore for the first time and reined the bronc around the corral in a wide turning maneuver. After completing a full circle, he eased to a halt and swung out of the saddle. The buckskin stood with its head bowed, sides heaving as it gasped for air.

Stillman retrieved his hat and dusted it off. He pulled the makings from his shirt pocket, rolling a smoke as he crossed the corral. One of the hands opened the gate and he sauntered outside, struck a match on his thumbnail. He lit up, smiling at Sontag.

"Got yourself a good mount," he said, snuffing the match. "'Course, he'll have to be topped off pretty regular."

"You're hired," Sontag said flatly. "We'll talk about wages later." He turned to the hands.

"Awright, quit lollygaggin' around. There's work to be done."

The men walked to their horses and mounted. Sontag led them out at a trot, riding west along the river. Slim Bohannon, the only one who remained behind, unsaddled the buckskin and led him back to the main corral. After closing the gate, he rejoined Stillman. His eyes crinkled with a smile.

"You plumb mortified the boss. He figured that hammerhead would haul your ashes."

Stillman puffed his cigarette. "One critter's pretty much like another. Lots of 'em try that fence trick."

"How long you been forkin' broncs?"

"Since Christ was a pup."

Slim wagged his head. "Well, don't let the old man short you on wages. He's cheap as dirt."

"Obliged for the advice," Stillman said. "What's your job around here, Slim?"

"This and that." Slim flexed a lanky leg. "Got my knee busted up in a horse spill. The boss put me to doin' chores till I mend."

"Took a few spills myself along the way. Who's the woman I saw watchin' from the house?"

"Old man's wife." Slim pursed his mouth. "Don't let him catch you eyeballin' her. He's spiteful as a rooster with one hen."

"Not suprisin'," Stillman said. "She looks to be considerable younger."

"Worse'n that," Slim grunted. "There's talk she fools around now and again. 'Course, I wouldn't vouch for it myself."

Stillman looked toward the house. He stiffened as a man stepped onto the porch and stretched his shoulders. They had never met, but the man had once been pointed out to him in Cheyenne. His name was Jud Holt and he worked as a "regulator" for the Cattlemen's Association. The title was a polite term for a hired gun.

"Who's that?" Stillman asked. "One of the family?"

"That there," Slim said, "is puredee trouble. Name's Jud Holt and he kills people for a livin'. Works for the Association."

"Sontag got problems with rustlers?"

"So he says."

"You don't sound too convinced."

"Guess I ain't," Slim said pointedly. "We haven't lost a cow since I don't remember."

"Why's he here, then?"

"Beats the hell outta me. The old man sent for him 'bout a month ago. Gave him a room up at the big house."

"What's he do with himself?"

Slim snorted. "Every mornin' he rides out and come sundown he rides back in. Where he

goes and what he does nobody knows. He
don't talk much."

Stillman took a long drag on his cigarette.
He exhaled, staring at the man on the porch.
For the first time since taking the case, he felt
he'd uncovered a solid lead. There were no
rustlers raiding the Lazy S, no reason to import
a hired gun. Yet that was precisely what Will
Sontag had done, with no ready explanation
for his actions. Unless Jud Holt had been imported for a totally different reason.

A man who killed for a living took work
where he found it.

SEVEN

The following morning a similar pattern developed. Will Sontag and the hands rode out at sunrise for the day's work. A short while later Jud Holt saddled his horse and rode off on the trail toward town. To all appearances, it was just another routine day on the Lazy S.

Stillman suspected that it was anything but routine. Overnight he'd gone out of his way to befriend several of the cowhands. After supper, when the crew returned to the bunkhouse, he had spun a few whoppers about his travels as a bronc buster. The hands were a rough lot, and they admired a man who regularly climbed aboard outlaw horses. Before long, though none of them realized it, he had them doing most of the talking.

A question here and there kept the conversation on track. He was searching for information that would confirm or dispel what he'd been told by Slim. The story he got, though it varied in the telling, was essentially the same. Nobody recalled the last time a Lazy S cow had been rustled. Jud Holt had shown up out of the blue, slightly more than a month past. He seldom spoke to anyone except the boss and Mrs. Sontag, and he'd proved to be a standoffish bastard. He rode out every morning and rode back late every afternoon, regular as clockwork. Nobody had the least notion where he went.

Nor was anyone dumb enough to ask. The Lazy S crew, no less than Stillman, was aware that Holt reported directly to the International Cattlemen's Association. Formed by Western stockgrowers, the International was composed of representatives from the various state and territorial associations. The purpose of the organization was to render summary justice on rustlers and horse thieves. Jud Holt and men like him were hired to travel about the country dispensing swift and certain punishment. Few people, including law officers, were so witless as to question their actions. Dead men, either hanged or shot, were their calling card.

For Stillman there was an ominous undertone to Jud Holt's presence. His first hunch had been that Sontag, operating on his own, might have imported the gunman for personal reasons. Holt was an assassin by trade, and bushwhacking men was all in a day's work. From that angle his appearance at the ranch fitted perfectly with Sontag's obsession. Who better to scare people out of the valley than an experienced killer? One who left no tracks and seemed to vanish into thin air after each murder. Sontag's ranch, remote and isolated, was an excellent staging point for the killings. And a perfect hideout for the killer.

But overnight Stillman began toying with another theory. The International Association was noted for its roughshod justice, ignoring state boundaries and all forms of jurisdiction. Their regulators were roving mercenaries, paid to travel anywhere and kill anyone marked for death. So the presence of their most feared gunman raised the more ominous question. What if the International was cooperating with Sontag? Suppose there was an organized program to assist large cattlemen in restoring open range? After all, some men considered settlers and rustlers to be birds of a feather. For men of little conscience, killing one was hardly different than killing the other. And the end result might once again bring open range to Tenbow Valley.

That morning when he'd watched Holt ride out, Stillman was tempted to follow. The thought occurred to him that Holt might be stalking another victim, planning a kill. But he had set aside the urge to follow, fearful of attracting attention to himself. The worst thing possible would be to arouse suspicion, particularly when he was still operating on theory. Far better to lay low until he'd uncovered something incriminating, hard facts. So he had gone to work on the string of raw stock in the main corral. None of the horses were real outlaws, and his years in a saddle enabled him to contend with their pitching and bucking. The balance of his day had been spent topping one bronc after another.

Late that afternoon, the Sontag woman walked down to the corral. From the bunkhouse talk Stillman had learned that her given name was Amanda. She was thirty-five or a little older, with raven hair and dark, curious eyes. Something about her walk, her bold manner, gave the impression that she liked men. She waited by the fence until Stillman dismounted from a dun gelding. When he opened the gate, she smiled, her eyes inquisitive.

"I'm Amanda Sontag," she said. "Since you're on the payroll, I thought we ought to get acquainted."

"Yes, ma'am," Stillman said, knuckling his hat. "Proud to meet you."

"Your name's Cliff—Cliff Jordan?"

"Yes, ma'am."

"Forget the 'ma'am,'" she said, arching her head. "I'm not that old yet . . . am I?"

"Well, uh . . ." Stillman pretended to falter. "No, I reckon you're not."

"I'll bet the boys in the bunkhouse gave you an earful. About me, I mean."

Stillman shrugged. "Told me you were a mighty fine lady. Guess that was about it."

"You liar," she said with a teasing laugh. "I know what they say!"

Stillman was saved by the sound of approaching hoofbeats. He glanced past her and saw Jud Holt ford the river, his horse lathered with sweat. Suddenly alert, he wondered why the gunman had run his mount so far, so fast. A moment later Holt skidded to a halt and stepped down. His features were taut, almost a grimace.

"Will back yet?"

"Why, no," Amanda Sontag said. "You look a sight. What's happened?"

"Somebody else got himself killed."

"Who?"

"I'll tell you later," Holt said sharply. "You'd better get back to the house. Will don't like you talkin' to the hands."

"To hell with Will—and you too!"

She turned abruptly and marched toward the house. Stillman wasn't quite sure what to make either of the exchange or her heated reaction. But he was vitally interested in hearing about the killing, the where and the who. He looked around to find Holt glaring at him.

"Word to the wise, bucko. Keep your distance from Sontag's wife."

"Whatever you say," Stillman agreed. "I tend to my own knittin'."

Holt stared at him. "Sontag tells me your name's Cliff Jordan."

"Six days a week and all day on Sunday."

"Don't get smart," Holt said. "That your real handle?"

"What d'ya mean?"

"Have you ever used another name—an alias?"

Stillman looked offended. " 'Course I never used an alias! That's a helluva question to ask a man."

"Where you from?"

"Why're you askin' all these questions?"

"Quit hedgin' and gimme a straight answer."

"Hell I will," Stillman said, feigning indignation. "You got no right nosin' around in my business."

"Listen close," Holt said roughly. "I'm a stock inspector for the Association. You know what's good for you, start talkin'."

"How do I know you're a stock inspector?"

"Goddammit, ask Sontag when he gets here! He'll tell you."

"Well . . ." Stillman paused, seeming uncertain. "Awright, what was it you wanted to know?"

"Where you from?"

"Here, there, and yonder. Feller in my line of work drifts around."

Holt studied him skeptically. "Where'd you work last?"

Stillman was prepared for the question. To play the role of a bronc buster he'd done his homework. "Circle C," he said, "just south of Rock Springs."

"How do I know you're tellin' the truth?"

"Get on your horse and ride down there and ask. Owner's name is Joe Carter."

"Yeah, that's so." Holt frowned, rubbing his jaw. "You're a far piece north of the Circle C. How come you took so long to find another job?"

Stillman spread his hands. "Only work when I need a fresh stake. Why bust your butt when you don't have to?"

"You stop off in Tenbow on your way here?"

"Don't much like towns. Unless I need supplies, I keep on movin'."

"How'd you find the Lazy S?"

"Took a fork in the road," Stillman said. "Nice thing about forks, they always lead somewheres."

Holt decided he was talking to a saddle-tramp. He motioned with a dismissive gesture. "I'm done with you. Go on back to work."

"Hold on a minute," Stillman countered.

"You got all your questions answered. Lemme ask you one."

"What's that?"

"You told Miz Sontag somebody got himself killed. Who was you talkin' about?"

Holt's expression turned abrasive. Before he could reply, he was distracted by the sound of hoof beats. Will Sontag rounded the bend in the river and rode toward the corral. A moment later he brought his mount to a halt. He dismounted, looping the reins over the top fence post. His gaze settled on Holt.

How come you're back so early?"

"Got some news," Holt said. "Another sodbuster was killed."

Sontag's mouth went tight. "Who?"

"George Blackburn, over on the Middle Fork."

"You're plumb certain, no mistake?"

Holt gave him an insolent look. "I don't make mistakes."

Sontag scowled, staring at the gunman. Then, abruptly, he became aware of Stillman standing there. His tone was harsh. "You waitin' on something?"

"Nope," Stillman said. "Just been answerin' questions for Mr. Holt."

Sontag muttered a curse. He glowered around at Holt. "I told you to stay clear of the hands."

"Keep your britches on," Holt said curtly. "I just thought I'd check him out."

"Don't think!" Sontag growled. "Do what you're told."

Their eyes locked in a tense silence. At length Sontag glanced at Stillman. "Unsaddle my horse and get back to work."

"Sure thing, Mr. Sontag."

Stillman tethered the bronc he was leading. As Sontag and Holt walked off, he moved to the rancher's horse and began loosening the cinch. He watched them over the top of the saddle and saw that they were engaged in a muffled argument. Sontag's voice suddenly rose in sharp anger.

"Why the hell'd you come back here? Your job ain't finished yet."

Holt's reply was too low to catch. Then they were out of earshot, striding toward the house. Stillman removed the saddle as Sontag stormed through the front door. Holt followed him inside.

Some moments later the sound of a bitter dispute drifted down from the house. Amanda Sontag's voice, higher in pitch, entered hotly into the argument. Stillman found himself puzzled by Sontag's anger, and he wondered why Holt had cross-examined him so intently. None of it dovetailed with his theory that Holt had been hired to perform the killings. But some-

thing stuck in his mind, intrigued him. A sting-
ing remark by Sontag, directed at Jud Holt.

Your job ain't finished yet.

Stillman went about his usual routine the next
morning. At first light he joined the other
hands at washbasins outside the bunkhouse.
When they trooped over to the cook shack, he
went along, taking a seat at a table large
enough for twenty men. He wolfed down flap-
jacks and beefsteak and thick coffee black as
pitch. The meal was designed to stick to a
man's ribs, and he ate heartily. He figured it
would have to last all day.

Sontag gathered with the hands outside the
corral at sunrise. When they rode out, Stillman
caught his bay and left it saddled behind an
equipment shed. Then he roped a bronc, led it
to the breaking pen, and hitched it to a post.
Afterward, as though preparing for the day's
work, he took his time inspecting the rigging
on a breaking saddle. All the time his eyes were
fixed on the main house.

Presently the door opened and Jud Holt
stepped outside. He walked directly to the corral, where he roped and saddled his chestnut
gelding. While he worked, Amanda Sontag
waited in the doorway of the house, watching
his every movement. He glanced once or twice
in her direction, as though irritated by her

scrutiny. Finished saddling, he rode by the breaking pen, staring straight ahead, offering no acknowledgment of Stillman's presence. After fording the river, he nudged his horse into a trot.

Stillman continued to fuss with the rigging. He silently cursed the Sontag woman as she stood in the doorway, watching Holt fade into the distance. Finally, when he could delay no longer, he hurried to the equipment shed and mounted his bay. When he rode past the corral, he saw Amanda Sontag move to the edge of the porch, staring at him in bewilderment. He cursed again, all too aware that his plan had gone haywire. Soon enough she would figure out where he was headed.

Far ahead, he saw Holt disappear around a stretch of timber. He forded the river, then gigged the bay into a hard lope. Having made the decision to trail the gunman, he couldn't risk losing him at the outset. Today, one way or another, he intended to find out where Holt went every morning. Events of yesterday, particularly the angry discussion between Sontag and Holt, had merely clouded the investigation. Whether or not they were involved in the killings would have to be determined by sunset at the latest. His undercover role at the Lazy S was now at an end.

Toward mid-morning, he halted on a

wooded rise. Below, the Middle Fork of the
Popo Agie curled through the valley. He dismounted, concealing the bay in the tree line,
and observed Holt reining up before a crude
log house. As Holt stepped down, a woman
with three small children clutching her skirts
appeared in the doorway. Holt doffed his hat
and began talking to the woman in an earnest
manner. She listened, her features stony and
suspicious, and finally nodded. She stepped
into the yard and pointed to a plowed field,
where a weeding harrow sat wedged between
rows. Then she pointed across the river to a distant hillside.

The woman suddenly broke down. She began sobbing and hugged her children as they
too started crying. Holt spoke to her, then
backed away, and mounted his horse. He rode
to the middle of the field and sat staring at the
harrow for a long moment. Finally he turned in
his saddle and scanned the distant hillside. He
seemed to be searching for something, looking
from the timbered hill to the harrow and back.
At last he reined his horse around and crossed
the field on a straight line. He forded the river
at a wide shallows.

As Stillman watched him, all of his doubts
were resolved. The woman was a new widow,
and the hard-scrabble farm was the homestead
of the sodbuster who had been killed yesterday.

Holt was clearly there to investigate the murder, which explained his daily absences from the Lazy S. Equally clear, for the past month Holt had been investigating the four previous murders. But understanding Holt's actions raised questions of greater complexity. Why would Sontag hire the Association gunman to track down a killer? Was there something more to the killings than a struggle for control of the valley? One question led to another and then another. A whole string of imponderables.

Holt searched the hillside for more than an hour. He walked it on foot, crisscrossed it on horseback, and rode circles around it. Quite obviously, he was trying to cut sign, locate day-old tracks in the hard earth. Yet his search was futile, and plain to see, he was not a skilled tracker. His blundering and thrashing, particularly on horseback, obliterated more sign than it uncovered. After a long while he stopped, took a look around, and then disappeared over the crest. From all appearances, he hoped to cut sign somewhere beyond the hill.

Stillman thought it an unlikely prospect. The tracks were a day old and the killer could have hightailed it toward many points on the compass. Worse, the tracks on the hillside were the tracks that would indicate the killer's general direction. And those tracks had now been destroyed in a careless search conducted too

quickly and without forethought. A month had
elapsed since Holt had started on the case, and
the reason he'd found nothing was all too apparent. He lacked the patience and doggedness
common to seasoned trackers. He would likely
blunder around in the mountains until night-
fall. And learn nothing for his efforts.

Stillman walked to the bay. He mounted and
swung wide of the field, crossing the river. He
had little expectation of finding anything, but
he thought it was worth a look. At the bottom
of the hill he left his horse hitched to an aspen
and proceeded on foot. The ground was a
patchwork of fresh hoofprints from Holt's hurried search. He started below the timberline
and began walking back and forth, on a direct
angle with the plowed field. He took his time,
scrutinizing the ground, covering the slope
step by step. By midday he was halfway up the
incline and yet to cut sign. Then, suddenly, he
stopped.

A glitter of sunlight bounced off something
metallic. He looked closer and saw a short
length of brass buried deep in a fresh hoofprint. Whatever it was, Holt's horse had
stepped on it and mashed it into the earth.
Squatting, he took a twig and gently pried the
object loose. As it broke free, he grunted softly,
staring at a spent rifle casing. He lifted it from
the earth, turning it to the light, and saw .50-90

stamped on the base. He realized he'd found a Sharps .50-90 cartridge.

Frozen, his eyes moved to a tree not three feet away. He studied the ground and slowly detected a slight depression just forward of the tree trunk. Another couple of feet down the slope he saw faded impressions of heel marks in the earth. A mental image abruptly formed in his mind's eye. He pictured the killer propped against the tree trunk, heels dug into the ground, braced in a sitting position. The Sharps steadied and a finger gently squeezed the trigger.

And the sodbuster dropped dead in the plowed field.

EIGHT

The courtroom was crowded. Several settlers garbed in rough clothing were seated toward the front. The remaining benches were occupied by curious townspeople. Civil trials rarely attracted large numbers of onlookers, but the case to be heard today was unique. No one had ever before sued Frank Devlin.

John Morton, one of the town's five lawyers, represented the plaintiff. Her name was Sarah Gortmann and she was attired in a worn print dress. She was the widow of Ernst Gortmann, who had been shot to death some six weeks ago. Her sons, aged ten and eleven, sat with neighbors directly behind the plaintiff's table. Simple farm people, they looked uncomfortable in such formal surroundings.

Frank Devlin arrived shortly before ten o'-clock, when proceedings were scheduled to get underway. The size of the crowd surprised him, and he looked momentarily perturbed. Then he regained his usual affable manner, nodding and smiling to acquaintances as he moved down the aisle. His suit was freshly pressed, and his overall appearance was that of a substantial businessman. With his attorney, William Archer, he took a seat at the defendant's table.

A door opened at the rear of the room. Judge Vance Taggart appeared and the bailiff called the court to order. The principals in the case, as well as the spectators, rose to their feet. Dressed in a somber black suit, the judge moved quickly to the bench and seated himself in a high-backed chair. He looked out over the crowd as the court clerk read the particulars of the legal action. Sarah Gortmann, the plaintiff, charged the defendant, Frank Devlin, with fraud.

"Plaintiff ready?" Judge Taggart asked. "Defense ready?"

"We are, Your Honor," Morton responded.

Archer half rose from his seat. "Defense is prepared, Judge."

"Before we commence," Taggart said sternly, "let me warn everyone that this court does not tolerate unruly behavior. Anybody gets out of line and I'll have you removed posthaste. Understood?"

The lawyers nodded and the crowd remained silent. Vance Taggart was an imposing man, tall and stately, with a sweeping mustache and gray hair. For twelve years he had served as county judge, and he ran his courtroom with an iron will. He presided over every legal proceeding in Fremont County, civil as well as criminal. His rulings were impartial but sometimes harsh, adhering to the letter of the law.

"Let's get started," Taggart said. "Plaintiff, call your first witness."

Sarah Gortmann took the witness stand. She was sworn in and seated herself in a straight-backed chair. John Morton approached, halting beside the empty jury box.

"Mrs. Gortmann," he said, "you have resided in this county for ten years. Is that correct?"

"Yes, sir," she replied. "My husband and me settled here in the spring of '68."

Morton led her through a series of preliminary questions. He established that she and her husband had homesteaded a quarter-section in the northwestern quadrant of Tenbow Valley. The farm prospered, they acquired legal title to the land, and raised two sons. He then directed her attention to the spring of 1878.

"On May 12 of this year, isn't it a fact that your husband was murdered?"

Sarah Gortmann's eyes teared. "Yes, sir, shot down with never a chance."

"And two days later," Morton said, pausing dramatically, "while you were still grieving your loss, you sold your farm to Frank Devlin. Is that correct?"

"Yes, sir," she said, darting a glance at the defense table. "He caught me at my wit's end and fast-talked me into selling the place."

"How much did he pay for your farm, Mrs. Gortmann?"

"Five thousand dollars."

Morton brought her now to the point at issue. In subsequent weeks two small ranchers and another farmer had been killed. Frank Devlin had bought out the widows, paying considerably more for their land rights. Sarah Gortmann alleged that he had defrauded her, underpaying current market value. She and her sons were living in town now, wholly dependent on their savings for a livelihood. She wanted fair value for her former holdings.

In a lengthy cross-examination, William Archer failed to rattle Mrs. Gortmann. She bitterly denounced his client, claiming she had been cheated during a moment of emotional suffering. When the examination was finished, he called Devlin to the stand. The land speculator testified that his intent had never been to defraud. Instead he'd offered a fair price, and Widow Gortmann had eagerly accepted. The price on subsequent land purchases, he con-

tended, was not relevant. Another party, Will
Sontag, had forced him into a bidding contest
for the properties. He'd actually overpaid fair
market value.

The trial had consumed the better part of
two hours. Judge Taggart, who believed in
swift justice, rendered an immediate decision.
Fair market value, he noted, was what buyers
were willing to pay at any given moment. For
Devlin to argue that he'd overpaid was patently
absurd. The three subsequent land deals had
instead established a more equitable market.
He ruled in favor of the plaintiff and ordered
Devlin to pay her an additional thousand dollars. Any motion for appeal, he announced,
would be heard after the noontime dinner
break. He then recessed court.

Devlin was visibly angered. In so many
words the judge had called him a swindler. Yet
he saw nothing to be gained by filing an appeal, which would require a court appearance
in Cheyenne. The delay, not to mention added
newspaper coverage, would further damage
his reputation in the community. He ordered
his lawyer to work out the details of payment
with the other side. For appearance's sake, he
attempted to speak with Sarah Gortmann. She
stared daggers at him and refused any conversation. His features flushed, he walked hur-
riedly from the courtroom.

Outside, Devlin started across the street. He met Lon Hubbard, the county sheriff, walking in the other direction. Behind him there was the murmur of voices as the spectators emerged from the courthouse. He saw the sheriff's eyes narrow in curiosity and knew he was about to be asked the outcome of the trial. The sheriff was an easygoing man and they were on good terms. But he hoped to avoid any discussion of the case, particularly under the amused stares of the courthouse crowd. He'd been embarrassed enough for one day.

Hubbard stopped directly in his path. Devlin slowed, prepared to make it a short conversation. Before either of them could speak, the boom of a heavy rifle echoed across the town. A moment passed, with Devlin and the sheriff and the courtroom spectators frozen in a stilled tableau. Then a woman's piercing scream broke the spell.

Judge Vance Taggart staggered around the far side of the courthouse. His shirtfront and coat were splotched with blood, and his arms were thrust outward, as though he'd been hurled forward by a fearsome blow. His feet tangled and he fell sideways, like a tree toppled from its roots. He struck the ground hard, skidding on his head in a puff of dust. One leg twitched, then he lay still.

Several men hurried forward from the courthouse steps. Devlin and the sheriff trailed close behind, and pushed their way through the crowd. The judge lay on his right side, one leg crooked at an odd angle, his eyes open in a death stare. Hubbard knelt down, turning the body, and cursed savagely. A ragged entry wound, ringed with blood, was centered between the dead man's shoulder blades.

Hubbard climbed to his feet. His gaze fixed on a hillside some five hundred yards to the rear of the courthouse. The crowd followed the direction of his stare, and the details were immediately evident. Judge Taggart had emerged from his chambers by a private side door and walked toward the front of the building. On the distant hillside someone firing a heavy-caliber rifle had shot him in the back. Mortally wounded, he'd then stumbled around the corner of the building and fallen dead.

"Gawdawmighty," Hubbard mumbled. "The bastard shot him at better'n a quarter mile."

"Just like the others," someone added. "Sonovabitch sure knows how to handle a rifle."

"No need to raise a posse," Hubbard said in a raspy voice. "He's long gone by now."

A silence fell over the crowd. They stood staring down at the blood-splattered body with a mix of anger and revulsion. Devlin eased through the crush of onlookers, moving toward the street. His features were rigid, his eyes curiously blank. He looked somehow drained of color as he set off downtown.

He suddenly wanted to find Monty Johnson.

Late that afternoon Stillman rode into the Lazy S. He unsaddled the bay and turned him into the corral. From the main house, he caught a face in a window and he knew he was being watched by Amanda Sontag. He walked toward the bunkhouse.

That morning, after finding the rifle shell, he'd been forced to a grudging admission. Neither Will Sontag nor Jud Holt were responsible for the killings. In fact, though the reason was unclear, it was now apparent that Holt was searching for the killer. Yet something about it didn't ring true.

For a good part of the afternoon he'd trailed Holt. His hope had been to somehow cut sign on the killer. But the terrain was stony and hard, and the only tracks he had seen were made by Holt's gelding. Finally he'd turned back, weary from what amounted to a lost cause. His thoughts went instead to the heated argument late yesterday, involving Sontag and his wife and Jud Holt. He was convinced that their argument revolved around the killer. Or perhaps Holt's failure to find the killer.

Thinking about it now, he wondered what they knew that he didn't. Even more, he wondered why they were frightened, what caused their fear. That was the only reasonable explanation as to why Holt had been imported. Sontag and his wife were afraid, and they'd hired the International's gunman to hunt down the killer. What he needed to know was the *why* behind their actions. Yet he couldn't ask without exposing his identity. Nor were they likely to answer, anyway. Whatever they were hiding, it was closely guarded. A secret shared only with Holt.

Slim appeared in the doorway of the equipment shed. He spotted Stillman and waited. "Howdy, Cliff," he said genially. "Where the deuce you been?"

"Nowheres much," Stillman said, evading the question. "Let's get washed up for supper."

"Lemme give you some free advice. Miz Sontag saw you ride out this mornin'. She asked me about it and I told her I didn't know nothin'."

"So what's the advice?"

"Get ready for a powwow with the boss. Soon as she tells him, he'll jump all over you. He's a stickler about a day's work for a day's pay."

Stillman was already aware that he had a problem. As yet he hadn't come up with a good excuse for his disappearance that day. He decided that he'd try to bluff his way through.

"Don't worry about it," Stillman said now. "I got my own deal with Sontag."

Slim appeared dubious. "Suit yourself," he said, then paused a moment. "Guess you ain't heard the news, have you?"

"What news?"

"There's been another killin'."

Stillman's look betrayed nothing. "Who's that?"

"Judge Taggart," Slim said. "County judge and one of the bigshots of Tenbow. Somebody drilled him outside the courthouse."

"How'd you hear about it?"

"Cook went into town for supplies this mornin'. He was there when it happened."

Stillman nodded. "They catch the killer?"

"Nope," Slim said, wagging his head. "Feller nailed him from a long ways off, just like the others. Got away clean."

"Any witnesses?"

"Half the gawddamn town! A widder woman took that land grabber to court, the one named Devlin. She won the case and they broke for dinner. That's when the fireworks started."

"Outside the courthouse?"

"Yep," Slim said. "Everybody and his dog saw the judge get it."

Stillman frowned. "Was Devlin there?"

"Well, shore he was. The judge had just ruled for Miz Gortmann and they all come out of the courthouse. They was standin' right there."

Stillman's head buzzed with questions. Why was the county judge the latest victim? Was there a link between the judge and the previous victims? Was Devlin somehow involved with the judge as well as the murdered landowners? Suddenly he knew that he wouldn't find the answers to these questions on the Lazy S. He had to return to Tenbow.

Westward along the river, he saw Sontag and several hands riding toward the compound. A moment later he caught sight of Holt riding in from the south. Sontag dismounted at the corral, waiting for Holt while the hands tended to their horses. Amanda Sontag hurried down from the house, pulling her husband aside and talking rapidly. When Holt arrived, the three of them huddled in low-voiced conversation. The woman kept nodding toward Stillman.

After several minutes Sontag sent his wife back to the house. Then he turned, motioning to Stillman with a rough gesture. Slim clucked something to himself and vanished into the equipment shed. Stillman walked forward, casually rolling himself a smoke. He struck a match on his belt buckle as he approached the two men. His features were unreadable.

"You want me?"

"Tell you what I want," Sontag said gruffly. "Why'd you light outta here this mornin'? Where you been all day?"

"Went for a ride," Stillman said without expression. "Haven't seen much of your spread since I hired on. Decided I'd have a looksee."

"You were hired to break horses. Anybody give you permission to go gallivantin' around the country?"

"I contracted to break 'em by the head. Don't reckon I need permission to take time off."

"The hell you don't!" Sontag exploded. "Anybody works for me, he does as he's told. You got that straight?"

Stillman crushed his cigarette underfoot. "Suppose you get my wages ready. I just quit."

"What d'you mean, quit? You still got stock to break."

"Let somebody else break 'em. Nothin' but a bunch of crowbaits, anyhow."

"Listen here—"

"Hold on," Holt interrupted, looking at Stillman. "Mrs. Sontag says you followed me out of here this mornin'. What's your story?"

"Never followed you," Stillman said lightly. "Why'd I do a thing like that?"

"Dammit, that's what I'm askin' you."

"Done told you I went for a ride."

"Bullshit!" Holt snarled. "Start talkin' or I'll slap you six ways to Sunday!"

Stillman smiled. "I reckon you could try."

Holt muttered an oath. Setting himself, he

launched a looping roundhouse punch. Stillman slipped inside the blow and buried his fist in the gunman's midsection. Holt's mouth opened in a soundless oval as air whooshed from his lungs. Shifting his stance, Stillman delivered a splintering left hook followed by a short right to the jaw. Holt went down as though his legs had been chopped off, and hit the ground with a dusty thud. He was out cold.

Sontag looked dumbstruck. He stared down at the gunman for a long moment, as though examining a natural disaster. Then he glanced up at Stillman.

"You're awful handy with your fists."

"Your boy ain't," Stillman said, maintaining the role of a tough bronc buster. "He oughta take lessons."

Sontag eyed him warily. "Who the hell are you, anyway?"

"I don't catch your drift."

"Something don't exactly set right. You're a little too cagey for my taste."

"Easy enough to solve that. Pay me off and I'll be on my way."

Ten minutes later Stillman rode out of the compound. Jud Holt sat where he'd dropped, a kerchief pressed to the bloody mess around his nose. Their eyes met and Holt stared at him with cold rage. Stillman had seen such looks before, the fury of a toughnut brought down a peg. He made a note to watch himself next time their trails crossed.

Something told him it was bound to happen.

NINE

The sun went down in a great splash of orange and gold. To the west the peaks of the Wind Rivers were momentarily bathed in flame. Then dusk quickly settled over the land, sunset replaced by shadows. The mountains loomed stark against a darkening sky.

Stillman reined to a halt. Ahead lay a fork in the winding road. One branch twisted off in an easterly direction, toward Tenbow. The other turned southward, a rutted trace that connected with the Middle Fork of the Popo Agie. He hesitated, staring at the Tenbow turnoff.

An hour ago, when he'd ridden out of the Lazy S, he had fully intended to head for town. But now, sitting motionlessly in the saddle, he weighed the alternative. Whatever was to be learned in Tenbow would wait until morning. Tonight he felt a growing need to talk with Carl

Richter, ask some hard questions. Things were not as he'd been told when he was hired.

The murder of Judge Taggart put a new face on the investigation. All the past killings had been directed at homesteaders and small ranchers. Their deaths appeared connected to the land and who coveted it most. Yet a county judge seemingly uninvolved in land disputes had been shot down. And the manner of his death indicated the handiwork of one killer, the same killer. The riddle had suddenly become more complex.

Deep in the woods, an owl hooted as dusk slowly turned to dark. The sound broke Stillman's moment of indecision, and he reined the gelding onto the southern branch of the road. From his meeting with Richter, he recalled that the rancher's spread was located on a tributary of the Middle Fork. The layout of Tenbow Valley was distinct in his mind, somewhat like a topographic map. The moon and stars were his compass, and direction, even at night, was almost second nature. He rode onward into the gathering dark.

Some residue of doubt still lingered. As a normal practice he stayed clear of the client once he'd accepted a case. What the client didn't know couldn't be repeated. So he usually kept his own counsel until the investigation was closed. There was as well a chance that the client hadn't been forthcoming at the out-set. Some people, for reasons of their own, pur-posely lied by omission, left certain facts unrevealed. At times it was a matter of faulty memory, or simple embarrassment at being in-volved. Other times it was intentional, and pos-sibly threatening, setting in motion events to achieve some hidden purpose. A detective soon learned to trust no one, clients included.

Stillman thought about that as he rode south. Before leaving Cheyenne, he'd made discreet inquiries about Carl Richter. From what he gathered, the rancher had been the second cat-tleman to settle in the valley, close behind Will Sontag. At one time his outfit had claimed most of the grazeland below the Middle Fork, a vast wilderness domain. And like Sontag, his cattle empire had shrunk to half its original size with the end of open range. Yet Richter was consid-ered an honorable man, decent and law-abiding. According to all sources, he bore no grudge toward the homesteaders and smaller ranchers. He was willing to live and let live.

Sometimes Stillman wondered if his work made him too cynical. Years of experience had taught him that no man's reputation was spot-less. The high and mighty were often as crooked and vengeful as common outlaws. Carl Richter might be as forthright as he looked and sounded, a man everyone admired. But then again, looks were deceiving and words were cheap. Some of the world's great grifters passed themselves off as church deacons.

Richter nonetheless deserved the benefit of the doubt. Stillman decided he would reserve judgment until they had talked. The rancher was probably as upright and trustworthy as he appeared, honestly shocked by the violence and death gripping the valley. Yet there were questions that needed asking and no two ways about the answers. No holdouts, no fudging the truth. Straight talk or else.

Late that night, Stillman sighted the ranch headquarters. A sallow half-moon lit the sky as he rode into the compound. The bunkhouse was dark and a single lamp burned in the main house. He dismounted out front, leaving the reins looped around the hitch rack. On the porch a mottled house cat watched him with wary eyes. He rapped on the door.

Footsteps sounded inside. The door swung open in a bright shaft of lamplight. Carl Richter peered out at him with undisguised amazement. "Stillman!" he said tentatively. "Where'd you come from?"

"You alone?"

"Well, yes," Richter said. "I was working on the account books. My wife's already gone to bed."

"We need to talk."

Stillman moved past him into the parlor. The furnishings were of hard wood and leather, made for comfort. A lamp spilled light over open ledgers on top of a sturdy desk. Grouped before the fireplace were a horsehair sofa, a rocker and a leather-backed chair.

"Here, sit down," Richter said, seemingly recovered from his surprise. "You're the last person I expected to come knocking on the door."

Stillman seated himself, dropping his hat on the sofa. "Thought I'd bring you up to date," he said. "I've just come from Will Sontag's place."

"Sontag?" Richter took the chair, his expression baffled. "You talked to Sontag?"

"After a fashion," Stillman remarked. "I hired out to break horses for him."

"I'll be damned," Richter said, impressed. "You really are a man of many parts, aren't you?"

Stillman saw no reason to impress him further. The role he'd played in Tenbow would for now remain privileged information. He subjected Richter to hard scrutiny. "Why didn't you tell me Jud Holt was working for Sontag?"

"I—" Richter faltered, lowered his eyes. "I was afraid you wouldn't take the job. Holt's got a bad reputation."

"So do I," Stillman said. "Especially when people lie to me."

"No harm intended. I should've told you."

"I take it personal when a man puts me in harm's way. You want me to spell that out?"

"No," Richter mumbled. "I understand."

"So what else did you lie to me about?"

Richter felt the full impact of Stillman's gaze. He swallowed, hastily licked his lips. "Nothing," he said, clearly shamed. "I'm not a liar, Mr. Stillman."

Stillman was inclined to believe him. There was a tense silence before he finally nodded. "Way I figure it, you thought Holt was the killer?"

"That's right," Richter admitted. "Sontag's just rotten enough to hire him."

"Well, you can set your mind at rest. Holt and Sontag are in the clear."

"What makes you so sure?"

"I trailed Holt most of the day. While we were gone, somebody else was killed."

Richter passed a hand across his face. "I know," he said. "I was in town when it happened."

"Why'd you go to town?"

"Business," Richter said, visibly upset. "Vance Taggart was an old friend, a fine man. I'd just come out of the bank when the shot was fired."

"Something's fishy," Stillman said. "Are you holding out on me?"

"What's that supposed to mean?"

"For openers, why kill a judge? What's he got to do with farmers and one-cow ranchers? Where's the connection?"

Richter shook his head. "Ever since it happened, I've been asking myself the same thing. But it doesn't make any sense."

"Yeah, it does," Stillman said firmly. "We just don't know whichaway or how. He wasn't killed for no reason."

"Maybe there's something," Richter said doubtfully. "Leastways, it's the only thing that occurred to me."

"What?"

"The judge was a strong supporter of the homestead law. And he was an outspoken opponent of Frank Devlin. That's why he ruled for the Gortmann woman this mornin'."

"Are you accusing Devlin?"

"Why not?" Richter insisted. "Devlin's the only one who's gained from these killings. And he knew the judge was gonna rule against him. Knew it before he ever walked into court!"

"Won't hold water," Stillman said. "Devlin was there when the gun went off. That's a pretty fair alibi."

"Is it?" Richter said, peering at him. "Devlin might've been there, but his bullyboy wasn't."

"Monty Johnson?"

Richter nodded. "Nobody saw hide or hair

of him. And he normally sticks to Devlin like a mustard plaster."

Stillman got to his feet. "Glad we had ourselves a talk. I'll have to take another looksee at Mr. Johnson."

"What do you mean, another looksee? How'd you know about Monty Johnson, anyway?"

"Tricks of the trade," Stillman said, smiling. "Now you see it, now you don't."

Richter looked vaguely confused. Stillman offered no further comment, shaking hands on his way out the door. After mounting, he turned the bay north along the road. The moon was high and he set a steady pace, for there were things yet to be done. Tricks of the trade.

Tomorrow, Duke Drummond would reappear in Tenbow.

Streetlamps cast dim shadows throughout the business district. The moon had heeled over and the town was shrouded in the inky darkness that precedes dawn. The streets were deserted.

Stillman paused at the edge of town. He placed the time at roughly four in the morning. That gave him an hour or less before Tenbow's early risers went about their business. To play it safe, he took the gold tooth from his saddlebags and slipped it into place. Should he happen across someone, no explanation would work without the tooth. He looked more the saddletramp than the gambler.

Once more he scanned the street. There was no one in sight and the buildings were still dark. He dismounted, waiting a moment longer, then walked his horse to the livery stable. The door creaked when he opened it, but he moved inside with no undue noise. Working swiftly, he got the bay into a stall without disturbing the other horses. He unsaddled, quickly stowed the gear away, and latched the stall door. As he walked forward, a lamp came on in the office.

The stable owner, who lived in a room behind the office, turned from lighting the lamp. Some noise had awakened him, and as he moved to the doorway, Stillman stepped behind a broad stanchion. The owner walked along the stalls and suddenly stopped toward the rear of the building. He and the bay stared at one another for a long moment, and he muttered something under his breath. Finally, shaking his head in disgust, he returned to the office. Yawning wide, he extinguished the lamp.

Stillman slipped through the front door. Outside, he hurried up the street to the hotel. A lamp burned low on the room clerk's desk, but the lobby was empty. He crossed to the stairs and quietly made his way to the second floor.

Once inside his room, he lighted the bedside lamp and began undressing. As he discarded clothing, it occurred to him that there was no need to rush. The sporting crowd rarely awoke before noon, and that was time enough for Duke Drummond to make an appearance. He turned back the covers, crawled into bed, and doused the lamp. His head touched the pillow and he fell into an exhausted sleep.

Some five hours later he awoke. After rolling out of bed, he checked his pocket watch and saw that it was almost ten o'clock. He took a bird bath in the wash basin, then poured fresh water, and shaved. A rumbling in his stomach reminded him that he hadn't eaten since yesterday. He dressed in his gambler's outfit and went down to the café near the hotel. The cook obliged him with ham and eggs, sourdough biscuits, and strong black coffee. On the street again, he felt ready for the day's business. He lit a cheroot, puffing smoke as he walked away.

Uptown, he headed toward Frank Devlin's storefront office. His plan was to wander past as though out for a morning stroll. The idea was to engage Devlin and Monty Johnson in conversation, and see where it led. He felt reasonably confident that he could draw them out, pose questions without appearing too inquisitive. The trick was to appear interested, but not press them beyond a certain point. Their reactions were the key far more so than their words. A man's expression, something about his eyes, invariably told the truth.

The office was modest. There was a single desk, three chairs and a file cabinet, and a large floor safe. When Stillman entered, Devlin looked up from behind the desk. Monty Johnson, who was seated in a chair against the wall, stared at him with an indifferent expression. Devlin greeted him with a wide smile.

"Here's the gamblin' man," he said. "We were talking about you just last night."

Stillman grinned. "Guess I'm a popular fellow around here."

"Talk of the town," Devlin said amiably. "Everybody was wondering where you'd gone."

"Business," Stillman said, flashing his gold tooth. "One of your local cattlemen invited me to a private game. Some people like to buck the tiger."

"Anybody I know?"

"Since he lost pretty heavy, I better keep my lip buttoned. He wouldn't appreciate word getting around."

"Come to think of it," Devlin said, "you've still got some of my money. When do I get a chance to win it back?"

"Matter of fact," Stillman said, "that's why I dropped by. Thought we might get a game together tonight."

"Suits me just fine. I'd even be willin' to raise the stakes."

"Now that you mention it, I heard you're a sporting man. That rancher told me you've been buying land all over the place."

"Did he?" Devlin looked proud of himself. "You ought to get into the land game yourself. Lots better odds than poker."

"Too fast for me," Stillman said. "Land speculation separates the men from the boys."

Devlin motioned to Johnson. "That's why I keep Monty on the payroll. I offer the best deal and I pay hard cash. You might say Monty rides shotgun."

Stillman took a thoughtful puff on his cheroot. "Around these parts, that makes sense. Way I hear it, there's a mad-dog killer on the loose."

"Sad thing," Devlin said, suddenly somber. "No rhyme or reason to it."

"Folks were talking about it over at the café this morning. Someone said you were there yesterday when the judge was shot."

"Half the town was there."

Stillman casually turned. "How about you?" he said to Johnson. "You see it, too?"

Johnson exchanged a quick look with Devlin. There was a question in his eyes, a moment of hesitation. Then his gaze shifted back to Stillman. "Didn't see nothin'," he said. "Everything was over when I got there."

Stillman sensed that a silent message of some sort had passed between the two men. As he turned to Devlin, he saw tension etched on the land speculator's features. He puffed a thick wad of smoke, feigned an offhand look of interest.

"Nobody was talking about anything else this morning. Have to admit, they got me to wondering, too."

Devlin took the bait. "Wondering what?"

"About the judge," Stillman said, idly waving his cheroot. "How's his death tie in with those other men that were killed? Everyone thinks it's damn peculiar."

For an instant there was a tightening around Devlin's mouth. Then he recovered, forcing a smile. "Death fascinates people," he said, "no doubt about it. Personally, I'm more interested in the here and now. What time you plan on startin' that poker game?"

"Anytime a'tall," Stillman said, laughing. "You name it."

"Hour or so after supper suit you?"

"Sounds made to order."

Stillman flipped them a mock salute. On his way out the door, he felt their eyes boring into his back. He knew he'd touched a nerve, shaken them. Their reaction told the tale.

Talk of murder made them nervous.

TEN

Stillman walked back to the hotel. On the veranda he took a seat in one of the cane-bottomed rockers. He needed time to digest what he'd learned from the conversation. Think it through and plan his next step.

The town had settled into its mid-morning routine. Stores were busy and a constant flow of passersby crowded the boardwalks. Wagons and men on horseback jammed the street, raising a curtain of dust. The scene was one of a prosperous community thriving on commerce and trade. There was a feeling of industry and purpose about the townspeople.

From the veranda Stillman watched them with no great interest. His thoughts were turned inward, sorting fact from conjecture. He had now verified what he'd been told last night by Carl Richter. Monty Johnson, by his own admission, had not been present when the judge

was shot. Which raised a question that had yet
to be answered. One that could not be asked
without arousing suspicion.

Where was Johnson when the killing took place?

A boy hawking newspapers wandered past
the hotel. Stillman bought a copy of the *Tenbow
Chronicle* and scanned the front page. The paper was a special edition with bold headlines
announcing the murder of Judge Vance Taggart. Fully half the front page was devoted to
the story, and there was a sidebar editorial. The
publisher of the paper railed and thundered
about the killings, charging the sheriff with
gross incompetence. The editorial ended with a
demand for immediate action.

Stillman considered that unlikely. A back-
country sheriff was generally capable of maintaining the peace and collecting taxes. There
were a few with the necessary experience to
track bank robbers and rustlers and occasionally arrest a wanted man. But the majority by
far lacked the skill required for an investigation
of any complexity. With six men dead and no
results to date, indications were that Sheriff
Lon Hubbard fell into the latter category. Solving murders was not his strong suit.

"Some story you're reading, isn't it?"

The voice brought Stillman around in his
rocker. He saw Tom Wexler, the hotel owner,

standing in the doorway. In passing they had exchanged greetings a couple of times in the lobby. But Wexler had evidenced no great curiosity about a gambler who would soon move on to another town. His question now gave Stillman an opening. One that might be turned to advantage.

"Helluva note," Stillman said, tapping the newspaper with a finger. "You'd think somebody would've caught this murderer by now."

Wexler chuckled. "Nobody ever mistook our sheriff for a Pinkerton man. Where murder's concerned, he's like a fish out of water."

"All the same, this doesn't take a mental giant. Six men dead ought to give a clue of some sort."

"Yeah, you'd think so," Wexler agreed. "Trouble is, Hubbard wouldn't know a clue if it spit on him. He's run himself ragged and got nowhere."

Stillman shook his head ruefully. "Terrible thing about the judge getting killed. Makes you wonder if anybody's safe."

"Damned if that's not a fact! No tellin' where the bastard will strike next."

"Funny you'd say that," Stillman observed. "Not ten minutes ago, I was talking to Frank Devlin about that very thing."

"Frank's of the same opinion, is he?"

"Not surprising after what happened yesterday. Told me he was right there when the judge got shot."

"Heard that myself," Wexler said. "Him and the Gortmann woman had just come out of court."

"Uh-huh." Stillman paused, apparently caught up in a moment of reflection. "Now, there's a curious thing."

"What'd you mean?"

"Well, I was just thinking about that Monty Johnson. He wasn't with Devlin at the courthouse yesterday. Leastways that's what he told me."

"So?" Wexler said. "I don't follow you."

Stillman shrugged. "From what Devlin says, Johnson's pretty much his shadow. Sort of a personal watchdog and bodyguard. Wonder where he was yesterday?"

Wexler looked at him oddly. "Hadn't really thought about it," he said, "but I saw Johnson come out of the Tivoli. Just after everybody started runnin' toward the courthouse."

"Devlin must've let him have some time off."

"More'n likely that's the case. Why're you so worried about Monty Johnson?"

"Professional curiosity," Stillman said, smiling. "You play poker with a man, it pays to know something about him. Especially when he's got a hard case standin' at his elbow."

"Who told you Johnson's a hard case?"

Stillman laughed. "Nobody had to tell me that. I know one when I spot him."

"Lemme tell you something," Wexler said, frowning. "Monty Johnson's tough, but I wouldn't put any labels on him. I've seen lots worse."

"Sounds like you and him are friends."

"Him and Devlin both," Wexler said levelly. "You're the stranger here, so take my word for it—Frank Devlin's the best thing that ever happened to this town."

"Are you talking about his land deals?"

"Let's just say he's gonna put Tenbow on the map."

Stillman attempted to draw him out further. But Wexler suddenly turned close-mouthed, as though he'd said too much already. He disappeared into the hotel and left Stillman to ponder his last statement. Which became something of an enigma when examined more closely. How, exactly, was Devlin going to put Tenbow on the map?

Yet that was a riddle for another time. Stillman's immediate interest had to do with Monty Johnson. By happenstance he'd stumbled across a piece of information. According to Wexler, Johnson had come out of the saloon moments after the shooting occurred. If that were true, then Devlin's watchdog ceased to be a suspect in the case. There was one way to find out.

Folding the newspaper, Stillman stuck it under his arm. He walked to the edge of the veranda and stood looking up and down the street. To all appearances, if Wexler was watching from inside, he seemed at a loss for what to do with himself. Finally, as though nothing better presented itself, he crossed the street and entered the Tivoli. Saloons generally maintained a fairly consistent work schedule. He was betting that the bartender from yesterday morning was on duty again today.

The barkeep wore red garters on his sleeves and a friendly smile on his face. Stillman ordered a beer and spread the newspaper on the counter. When the bartender returned with a foaming mug, he dropped a silver dollar on top of the newspaper. As the barkeep reached for the coin, he nodded to the headline set in bold type.

"Quite a town," he said, hefting the mug. "Gettin' to be a regular shooting gallery."

"Goddarned shame and that's a fact! I voted for Judge Taggart last election."

"Heard you had a crowd when it happened. Place must've emptied out pretty fast."

The barkeep's forehead wrinkled in concentration. "We wasn't all that busy," he said. "The noontime crowd hadn't come in just yet. I only recollect a couple of customers."

"Early drinkers," Stillman prompted. "Hair of the dog to settle their stomachs from the night before."

"Not them two," the barkeep said. "Charlie Thomas, from up at the notions store, was one. And the other was that Johnson feller, works for Mr. Devlin. He's just a sipper, strictly beer."

Stillman seemed to lose interest. "What time does Jennie start work?"

"Five or thereabouts. Not much action before then."

"Tell her Duke Drummond was asking."

"Yessir, Mr. Drummond, I shorely will."

The barkeep went to make change for the nickel beer. Stillman took a long slug and wiped foam off his mustache. Somehow the information left him unsettled rather than convinced. An hour ago he'd been reasonably confident that Devlin and Johnson were involved in the killings. But now, with what he'd learned, that appeared unlikely. Perhaps downright impossible.

They both had ironclad alibis.

Stillman spent the balance of the day in his hotel room. Having eaten a late breakfast, he decided to forgo the noonday meal. His mind was

on matters other than food, and none of his
thoughts was reassuring. He'd once again hit
an impasse.

Hard realities were difficult to accept. Yet he
was forced to admit that the investigation was
stymied. For all intents and purposes, the major suspects in the case had been cleared. There
was no doubt that Will Sontag, aided by Jud
Holt, was actively searching for the killer. The
reason for their search was still a moot question, and they were unlikely to volunteer information. So the answer might never be known.

Nor was there anything of a positive nature
with respect to Frank Devlin. Something about
the man was definitely not as it appeared. No
one bought land and held on to it without a
purpose. But his strange business practices
were in no way incriminating; apart from land
purchases, he was scarcely connected to the
murders. Even his bodyguard, Monty Johnson,
had turned out clean. Neither of them could be
implicated.

The tangled skein of the case left Stillman
baffled and angry. He had no doubt whatever
that more people were slated for death. He was
convinced that the killings were not random
murders performed by some madman gone
berserk. Somewhere within the brutal deaths
there was a pattern, a common thread. The
man who pulled the trigger was selecting his

victims, effectively assassinating people in
some unrevealed order. Yet there was nothing
to indicate his identity or his motive.

Stillman mentally reviewed what he knew of
the killer. The weapon used was a Sharps rifle,
favored by buffalo hunters for its power. The
killer was a highly proficient marksman,
deadly accurate at long range. From the scant
evidence available, he was also versed at covering his tracks, and no greenhorn in the wilderness. He was like a phantom, vanishing into
the mountains after every killing. All of which
pegged him as a seasoned outdoorsman, even a
skilled hunter. And none of which fitted the
prime suspects in the case.

The thing that galled Stillman the most was
his sense of impotence. He was powerless to
prevent the killings yet to come, somehow
break the pattern and alter what seemed in-
evitable. His every instinct told him that more
people would die. Yet he could only wait until
they were shot down, and hope that the killer
made a mistake. Unless he was on the spot,
with a fresh trail to follow, there was small likelihood that he would ever crack the case. Waiting for people to be killed left a foul taste in his
mouth.

A knock sounded at the door. He warned
himself to be on guard as he crossed the room.
No one had reason to visit him, and he was

wary of unannounced callers. His hand went
to the holstered Colt and he positioned himself sideways to the door. When he opened it,
his immediate reaction was one of surprise.
The man standing in the hallway wore a star
on his vest.

"Afternoon," he said. "Are you Duke
Drummond?"

"Yes."

"I'm Sheriff Hubbard. Like to talk to you a
minute."

"Sure, come on in."

Lon Hubbard was a rawboned man somewhere in his late thirties. Without the badge he
might have been mistaken for a farmer or an
aging cowhand. But as he moved through the
doorway, Stillman was instantly on guard.
Something about his manner indicated that this
was not a courtesy call. He looked all business.

Stillman closed the door. "What can I do for
you, Sheriff?"

"Want to ask you a few questions."

"Go ahead."

Hubbard appeared uncomfortable. "Just doing my duty, you understand. A stranger draws
attention in a small town."

Stillman smiled. "Somebody accuse me of
something?"

"Not exactly," Hubbard said. "Got a report
you were out of town for a couple of days. Fact

is, I was told you sneaked out of town and sneaked back in. Anything to it?"

"I left at night and I returned at night. What's wrong with that?"

"Nothin', so long as you can account for your whereabouts."

"Why should I?"

"Because two men were murdered while you were gone. What you might call a coincidence."

Stillman was stunned. The logic of it made perfect sense. He was a stranger, and his unexplained disappearance naturally made him suspect. For a moment he considered revealing his identity to the sheriff. Yet he knew Hubbard would talk, and once the secret was out, any chance of operating undercover would vanish. The investigation would end and the case would never be solved. He decided to bluff it out.

"Wait a goddamn minute!" he said loudly. "Are you accusing me of killing those men?"

"Nope," Hubbard said. "Just wanna know your whereabouts when they was shot."

"Hell, Sheriff, you already know! Whoever owns the stable told you about me leaving town. And Frank Devlin probably told you I was involved in a private poker game."

By Hubbard's reaction he sensed he'd guessed right on both counts. The lawman hesitated a moment, then shook his head. "I still gotta know where you were."

"That's confidential information, Sheriff. Unless you're prepared to press charges, I don't have to tell you a damned thing."

"I oughta arrest you," Hubbard said sternly. "You're too much of a mystery man to my way of thinkin'."

"Sheriff, you're talking to the wrong man. We both know you'd never make the charge stick."

"Lemme give you some free advice. Watch your ass and don't try any funny tricks. I'll have my eye on you."

Hubbard walked out. Stillman understood he'd been put on notice. Hereafter his movements would be closely monitored, every action scrutinized. By sheer quirk he'd become both the hunter and the hunted. For the sheriff was now convinced that he was the chief suspect.

Perhaps the only suspect.

After supper, Stillman wandered over to the Tivoli. The men ganged around the bar fell silent, and he figured they'd heard the news. Word spread fast in a small town, particularly with a sheriff who liked to talk. Earlier, he'd decided to play it loose and rough. Anybody who spoke out of turn would be challenged on the spot. A bold front and a firm hand.

Jennie Blake intercepted him before he reached the bar. She took his arm and walked him to one of the tables at the rear. When they were seated, she leaned closer and kept her voice low. Her features were strained.

"You're in trouble," she said quickly. "Everyone thinks you had something to do with those killings."

"Don't worry about it," Stillman said. "That newspaper editorial lit a fire under the sheriff. He's just trying to make himself look good."

"Are you saying there's nothing to it? He's not going to arrest you?"

"Not unless he wants to make a fool of himself."

"Well, that's a relief!" She paused, then suddenly looked miffed. "Why the hell didn't you tell me you were leaving town? I thought I'd never see you again."

"What gave you that idea?" Stillman said, playing along. "You're the best thing Tenbow's got to offer."

"And you've got a gift for gab a yard wide! You probably came back just to trim some more suckers."

"Speaking of which, I invited Frank Devlin for a game tonight. Let me ask you something about him."

She batted her eyelashes. "Sweetie, I'll tell you anything you want to know. But don't you run out on me again. Promise?"

"Where would I run?" Stillman said evasively. "We're partners, aren't we?"

"All right, then, ask away."

"What do you know about Devlin before he showed up here? Where he came from? What line of work he was in? Anything at all."

She considered a moment. "When he first came here, I remember somebody asked him where he was from. He sort of stuttered around and finally said Rock Springs. I got the idea it was a slip of the tongue."

"Rock Springs," Stillman repeated to himself. "Anything else?"

"Not that I recall. He's pretty slick that way. Never gives you a straight answer."

"Well, that's more than I knew before."

"What's it got to do with poker?"

"I'll let you know when I find out."

Later that night, Stillman got his chance. Devlin and four other men joined him at the poker table. No one mentioned the killings, and Devlin made no reference to his talk with the sheriff. They concentrated instead on their cards.

Toward midnight, the deal passed to Devlin. As he began shuffling, Stillman worked the conversation around to the subject of big money games. He casually mentioned one he'd played in just a couple months ago down in Rock Springs. Out of the corner of his eye he saw Devlin's hands stop for an instant, then quickly resume shuffling. Glancing up, he found Monty

Johnson staring straight at him. He thought it was one of those looks that could kill.

Stillman knew he'd stumbled onto something. What it meant or where it would lead was another riddle added to a growing collection. But he had nothing better to do, and he was reluctant to sit around waiting for the next killing. So he made a snap decision.

Tonight, Duke Drummond would vanish again.

ELEVEN

The livery stable was dark. Working quietly, Stillman saddled the bay and led him out of the stall. None of the other horses were disturbed, and no lights came on in the office. He opened the front door only wide enough for the bay to squeeze through.

Once more he'd chosen to depart town in the dead of night. The hour was approaching two o'clock and the streets were empty. Overhead, a half-moon bathed the landscape in a dull glow. He paused a moment in the doorway, took a last look in both directions. Nothing stirred and he led his horse outside. The door closed with a muted creak.

Earlier, he had considered waiting until morning to leave town. But he'd quickly discarded the idea as unworkable, possibly risky. He was now a suspect in the killings, and the news had spread through Tenbow. Should he

attempt to leave town openly, he felt certain the
sheriff would arrest him. The charge might be
murder, or it might be some trumped-up charge
simply to prevent him from leaving. The mood
of the town was such that the people would
support any action taken by the sheriff. All the
more so since there were no other suspects.

By leaving at night he knew those suspicions
would be reinforced. Nonetheless, he saw that
as a calculated risk, one he had to accept. The
alternative was to chance being arrested and
held in jail until a court hearing could be scheduled. One thing worked in his favor: that day
he had paid another week for his hotel room as
well as the stable. Having done so indicated
that he planned to stick around awhile longer.
The sheriff would be furious, and when he returned to town, some reasonable explanation
would be needed to cover his absence. But he'd
decided to worry about that later.

For the moment the important thing was to
get clear of town. Frank Devlin, so far as he
could determine, was not directly responsible
for the killings. Yet there was a possibility that
Devlin had hired someone other than Monty
Johnson to perform the murders. The theory
gained credence from the fact that Devlin was
probably involved in an underhanded land
scheme of some nature. Details about Devlin's
background, and perhaps the land scheme,

might be found in Rock Springs. Devlin was obviously hiding something; the mere mention of Rock Springs had rattled his nerves. So that made it the logical place to look.

Stillman figured the trip would consume the better part of a week. Rock Springs was ninety miles or more southwest of Tenbow. By pushing it, he could travel there and return in a matter of six days. He knew the town marshal, and he'd already decided to trade on an old friendship. He felt whatever was to be learned in Rock Springs could be uncovered in a day's time, perhaps less. And what he learned might yet link Devlin to the killings, particularly if the land scheme was somehow outside the law. The thing that bothered him most was that he would be gone for nearly a week. Should the killer strike again while he was away . . .

The thought nagged at Stillman even now. Yet it was borrowing trouble, worrying about something that might or might not happen. As he gathered the reins to mount, he put it aside, forced himself to concentrate on getting out of town undetected. He stuck his foot in the stirrup and in the same split second a bullet fried the air past his head. Up the street, from a dark alleyway, he saw the fiery muzzle blast as the gunshot echoed through town. Gripping the reins in one hand, he pulled his Colt as a second slug plucked at the sleeve of his gun arm.

He triggered three shots in a staccato roar, aiming at the muzzle flash. His assailant suddenly quit the fight.

Stillman started toward the alley, then stopped. He heard the pounding thud of running footsteps growing steadily fainter. A lamp came on in a house up the street, and he knew the entire town would be aroused within minutes. He knew as well that there was virtually no chance of catching his assailant in the dark. To delay would achieve nothing, except certain arrest by the sheriff. He swung aboard the bay.

Someone shouted up the street as he gigged his horse into a lope. A moment later he disappeared into the night outside town. Along the south road, his recollection of the gunfight abruptly took form. The bushwhacker had fired a pistol, not a rifle! Which pretty much eliminated the killer who operated from long range. Instead, somebody from town had tried to kill him. Somebody who wanted him stopped tonight.

A full answer would have to await his return. But he recalled earlier, during the poker game, the look Monty Johnson had given him when he mentioned Rock Springs. He thought he knew who'd fired the shots.

Rock Springs was a major railhead in western Wyoming. The Union Pacific tracks drifted southwesterly, crossing the Green River and on into Utah. The railroad, and the coal mines that fed the locomotives, provided the economic base for a prosperous community. The town in large degree existed to serve the Union Pacific.

Stillman dismounted outside the marshal's office. He tied the bay to a hitch rack and spent a moment swatting trail dust off his clothes. His jawline was covered with a two-day beard, but otherwise he looked himself. The gold tooth was tucked away in his saddlebags.

Orville Brandt was town marshal of Rock Springs. His was an elected post, and he'd been returned to office every autumn for eleven years. He gave troublemakers a choice between obeying the law or a busted head and a stiff fine in city court. He was an old-time lawman, traveling from town to town as the railroad expanded westward. He'd finally put down roots in Rock Springs.

When Stillman came through the door, Brandt greeted him with a warm handshake. There was a kinship between them that went back to Stillman's days as a federal marshal. A part of that kinship stemmed from a shared belief that laws were made to be enforced. Their mutual respect was that of one strong man for another. Neither of them ever stepped back from trouble.

"Gawddamn, Jack!" Brandt whooped. "How long's it been?"

"Couple of years," Stillman said. "Summer of '76, just after Custer tangled with the Sioux. I was after a train robber."

"What happened when you caught him?"

"Dumb sonovabitch decided to fight."

Brandt roared with laughter. "Bend 'em or bury 'em, that's the motto! Glad to see you haven't changed."

"You look pretty much the same yourself."

"A little older but not a helluva lot smarter. Just take it a day at a time."

Brandt motioned to a chair, then seated himself behind the desk. He studied Stillman's bearded features and dusty clothes for a moment. "What brings you to Rock Springs?" he asked. "Even money says it's not a social call."

"I'm looking for information," Stillman said. "Character by the name of Frank Devlin. You ever hear of him?"

"Hear of him!" Brandt bellowed. "I chased the sorry bastard out of town. Less'n six months ago."

"What was he charged with?"

"Shady land deals," Brandt said. " 'Course, I never brought a formal complaint. He's too slick for that."

"So you just posted him out of town?"

"Yeah, that's about the size of it."

Stillman's gaze narrowed. "What kind of land deals?"

"Devlin's a sharpie," Brandt remarked. "Specialized in swindling broke sodbusters into signing quitclaim deeds. Then he'd palm the land off on some pilgrim for twice what it's worth."

"Skirted the law but never went over the edge, is that what you're saying?"

"You know how I work, Jack. Grifters and such aren't tolerated in my town. Only one message they understand: Get out or get your head busted."

Stillman nodded. "What about a tough item calls himself Monty Johnson? Was he involved with Devlin?"

"Oh, hell, yes," Brandt grunted. "Showed up here with him and left with him. Way it looked, they'd been together a long time."

"You ever have trouble with Johnson?"

"When I posted them out of town, he tried to give me some lip. Devlin told him to keep his trap shut."

"Any idea where they operated before they showed up here?"

Brandt shook his head. "Never bothered to check 'em out. Crooks are crooks, so why waste time?"

Stillman was silent for a long moment. Brandt looked at him with a quizzical expression. "You gonna tell me why you're askin' all these questions?"

"Devlin's rigged another land game. I was hired to investigate."

Brandt knew he hadn't heard the entire story. But he understood as well that his friend never discussed the details of a case in progress. He was not offended by the short answer. "Well, you got me to wonderin', so give it to me straight. You had any trouble with Johnson?"

"Night before last," Stillman said, "he took a couple of shots at me. Never saw his face, but I'd lay odds it was him."

"Then he was damn well followin' orders. He don't take a piss without first askin' Devlin."

"I had it figured the same way. Anything else you can tell me about them?"

"No-o-o," Brandt said slowly. " 'Course, you might talk to Art Muller, over at the Union Pacific. Devlin fooled him good there for a while."

"How so?"

"Devlin passed himself off as an experienced land agent. Told Muller he'd worked with the Kansas Pacific, selling right-of-way land to immigrants. He wanted to do the same for the Union Pacific."

"Likely story," Stillman said sardonically. "Did Muller hire him?"

Brandt uttered a sharp laugh. "Muller's no

dummy. He wired the Kansas Pacific and they'd never heard of Devlin. That was the end of that."

"What happened then?"

"Devlin went into business for himself. Started buying out homesteaders who were down on their luck."

"These homesteaders," Stillman inquired, "were any of the men killed before Devlin offered to buy the land?"

"Nope," Brandt said, looking at him strangely. "Have there been killings in the case you're workin' on?"

"Some folks think so."

"Well, for my money, Devlin's not above murder. 'Course, it'd be Monty Johnson who does the dirty work."

Stillman rubbed the stubble along his jawline. "While they were here," he said, "was Johnson ever involved in any gunplay? Any rough stuff at all?"

"Not that I know of," Brandt replied. "But you said he tried to put your lights out. That oughta tell you something."

"Yeah, but does it tell me enough?"

"I don't follow you."

"Just thinking out loud, Orville."

Their conversation ended shortly. Brandt walked him to the door and they shook hands. Outside, Stillman stopped to light a cheroot, reflecting a moment on what he'd learned. The gist of it squarely pegged Frank Devlin as a scoundrel, one capable of murder.

That left the question of why he'd set up shop in Tenbow.

Stillman went directly to a barber shop. There he got a shave and took a bath in the back room, soaking away the grime in a large, steaming tub. Afterward, refreshed and smelling of bay rum, he stepped into a café. He ordered steak and eggs, and drank three cups of coffee. All the while he was thinking about his next stop.

A short time later he left his gelding hitched outside the train station. The division offices of the Union Pacific were located on the second floor of the depot. Upstairs, he announced himself to a clerk and asked for Arthur Muller, the division chief. After a brief wait he was ushered into a corner office.

Art Muller was thin and balding, with spectacles perched on the end of his nose. He greeted Stillman with a loose handshake and a diffident smile. His retiring manner was deceptive, for he was noted as a shrewd administrator. His responsibilities encompassed all Union Pacific operations in western Wyoming. He offered Stillman a chair.

"Well, now, Jack," he said. "No one notified me you'd been retained."

"I haven't," Stillman told him. "I'm here on another matter."

"Pertaining to what?"

"Frank Devlin."

Muller's bony cheeks flushed. His hand darted in a reflex action to the spectacles. "What about Devlin?"

"For openers," Stillman said, "I had a talk with Orville Brandt. He says you had some business dealings with Devlin."

"Business!" Muller sputtered. "That overstates the case by far. I had a few discussions with him, nothing more."

"Way I heard it, he wanted to sign on as a land agent with the Union Pacific."

"Orville Brandt doesn't know what he's talking about."

Stillman looked skeptical. "Suppose you set me straight, then."

"The fact is—" Muller paused, cleared his throat. "Devlin claimed to have worked with the Kansas Pacific as a contract agent. Are you familiar with the term?"

"Not exactly."

"A contract agent is not an employee of the railroad. He contracts to sell land granted to the railroad as part of its right-of-way. Usually at an established price per acre."

"So he works for himself," Stillman said. "How does he get paid?"

"The customary arrangement involves a commission on anything he sells."

"Are there ways a contract agent could cheat on the deal?"

Muller blinked behind the spectacles. "Why do you ask that?"

"Simple," Stillman said. "Frank Devlin's a crook."

"What's your interest in Devlin?"

"You answer my question first."

"Well, yes," Muller said cautiously, "contract agents have been known to bend the rules. One way is to charge the buyers a cash fee for particularly desirable land."

"A hidden fee?" Stillman asked. "Over and above what's paid to the railroad?"

"That's correct."

"Let's say there's a piece of land with a good stream. The agent pockets what amounts to a bribe from the buyer. That the way it works?"

"Exactly."

Stillman considered. "So what made you suspicious of Devlin?"

"I'm not sure." Muller fidgeted with some papers on his desk. "Perhaps the fact that he was such a smooth talker. He just seemed too . . . polished."

"Was that why you had him checked out?"

Muller squirmed in his chair. His hand again fluttered to his glasses and a nervous tic pulled at the corner of his mouth. Watching him, Stillman sensed that he was burdened with some enormous guilt. He looked like someone in need of a confessor.

"Listen, Art, I'm not here to cause you trouble. Anything you say won't get beyond this room."

Muller appeared shaken. "Jack—" he hesitated, then rushed on. "I'd get fired if this ever came out. Lose my job, my pension, everything."

"You've got my word it stops here."

"I was a damn fool," Muller groaned. "He buttered me up and played on my vanity . . . and I finally told him."

"Told him what?"

"Company secrets," Muller said shakily. "We're going to reopen the line to South Pass City. The plans are in the works now."

"What the hell for?" Stillman said. "It's a ghost town."

"South Pass City means nothing. Our interest is in running a spur line from there to Tenbow."

"Tenbow?"

"Yes, indeed," Muller confirmed. "Tenbow Valley represents a potential bonanza for the railroad. With the farm community developing there—not to mention the ranchers—we foresee a very profitable market."

"I'll be damned," Stillman said, somewhat

amazed. "And you told Devlin the whole thing?"

"I'm afraid so," Muller said with a hangdog look. "At first I was really impressed with him. I thought he was the perfect man to represent us in Tenbow. But later, after I'd contacted the Kansas Pacific—"

"You found out he's a phony."

"Absolutely unscrupulous! An out-and-out fraud."

Stillman left the office with a renewed sense of purpose. He at last had the answer to the riddle of Frank Devlin. Tenbow Valley was about to become a rail center, and land prices would skyrocket. Which made it a virtual money tree for a land speculator who bought cheap before the news was made public. A fortune for the taking, worth any risk.

Worth lying and cheating, and murder.

TWELVE

The jail cell was small and cramped. Stillman lay stretched out on a lumpy cot, hands locked behind his head. A tendril of smoke drifted upward from the cheroot wedged in the corner of his mouth. Dull light streaming through the barred door caught the gleam of his gold tooth. He stared at a spot on the ceiling.

There was a certain irony to the situation. Thinking about it, he saw that he had no one to blame but himself. Last night he had returned to Tenbow in the early morning hours. With his usual stealth he'd made it to his hotel room and gone to sleep. Some hours later, he had been awakened by a banging on the door. When he opened it, Sheriff Lon Hubbard and a deputy were standing in the hallway. He'd been arrested for murder.

Marched off to the county jail, Stillman had been informed of the gravity of the charge. A small rancher had been killed west of Tenbow during his six-day absence. Last time he'd been out of town, the sheriff declared, a farmer and a county judge had been murdered. Three killings, all of which occurred when he couldn't account for his whereabouts, represented something more than coincidence. The sheriff demanded an explanation and he had refused. He'd been locked in a cell to think it over.

Stillman saw now that he should have foreseen the problem. Even before he left Tenbow, he'd been concerned that someone else would be murdered. The sheriff was under pressure to produce a killer, and he'd already been tagged as the prime suspect. Yet under questioning this morning, he had again hesitated to disclose his identity. Should the situation become critical, he was confident Carl Richter would back his story. For that matter, a wire to the U.S. marshal in Cheyenne would confirm that he had been hired to investigate the murders. But those were steps he looked upon as the last extreme.

For the moment he felt it was vital that he maintain his charade. The information he'd unearthed in Rock Springs seemed to him a strong indictment of Frank Devlin. Having learned of the railroad's plans, Devlin had come to Tenbow and established himself as a reputable land speculator. To scare people into selling, it followed that he would have orchestrated the string of murders. By buying cheap, he could wait for the spur line to be built and then reap enormous profits. While hard evidence was scarce, the case was nonetheless compelling. Lives were being sacrificed for land.

All things considered, Stillman saw no alternative to the undercover role he'd been playing. He now suspected that Tom Wexler, the hotel owner, might be involved with Devlin. Wexler had made a slip-of-the-tongue statement, to the effect that Devlin would put Tenbow on the map. At the time it made no sense, but now, in light of the railroad's plans, it indicated that Wexler had prior knowledge of Devlin's scheme. Perhaps there were others in town who had been secretly enlisted by Devlin. A conspiracy might exist, involving practically anyone motivated by greed. So there was no one who could be trusted.

Nor was there any rush to expose Devlin's scheme. The important thing was to catch the killer, avoid further loss of life. Stillman was no longer persuaded by Monty Johnson's alibi on the day of the judge's death. Wexler, who was party to the alibi, might have lied because of his involvement. The bartender at the Tivoli, who also verified the alibi, might have been paid to lie. He wanted to question them again, push them to the wall and see if their stories changed. There was no doubt in his mind that Johnson had tried to kill him outside the stable. Add that to a broken alibi, and Johnson became the logical suspect. Devlin's jack-of-all-trades, including murder.

But first Stillman had to somehow clear himself. So long as he was locked in a jail cell, he couldn't question anyone. He was mulling over the problem when Lon Hubbard appeared in the corridor. The sheriff unlocked the door and swung it open. He motioned Stillman outside.

"Let's go," he said. "Somebody wants to talk to you."

Stillman moved into the corridor. Hubbard fell in behind him and they walked toward the front office. Waiting for them was a stocky man, rather distinguished in bearing, attired in a somber cutaway coat and striped trousers. He watched without expression as the sheriff roughly seated Stillman in a chair. Then, hands clasped behind his back, he stepped closer.

"I'm Samuel Packard," he said, "the county prosecutor. Sheriff Hubbard tells me you've refused to cooperate."

Stillman smiled. "The sheriff wants me to confess to a whole bunch of murders. That's not my idea of cooperation."

"Suppose we try another tack. On separate occasions you've disappeared from sight when three men were murdered. How do you explain that?"

"Don't have to explain it," Stillman said. "You haven't got an iota of proof against me. I'm in the clear."

"Hardly, Mr. Drummond." Packard's voice was laced with sarcasm. "We have every reason to believe you've killed seven men. All we have to establish is the motive."

"What you have to establish is my guilt. We both know you can't do that. Otherwise you wouldn't be here. You'd be asking a grand jury for an indictment."

"You seem to know a great deal about the law."

"Look here," Stillman said. "Why don't we put our cards on the table? Save everybody a lot of grief."

"I'm a good listener," Packard said unctuously. "What's on your mind?"

"Do you have any witnesses to these killings?"

"Anyone who reads the paper knows the answer to that."

"Anybody who could identify me? Swear under oath I'm your man?"

"Not yet," Packard noted with a wry smile. "We expect someone to come forward at any moment."

"Horseapples," Stillman said bluntly. "That's pure bluff. Not too well done, either."

"Well, I haven't your experience at the gaming tables, Mr. Drummond. But I do have you—in jail."

"I suppose you've already searched my hotel room."

"Of course."

"Anything dawn on you when you checked my rifle?"

Packard exchanged a glance with the sheriff, who shook his head. "That proves nothing," Packard said. "You might have a larger caliber rifle hidden somewhere."

"You've got things bassackward," Stillman informed him. "You're the one that has to come up with proof. And the way I hear it, you're whistling in the dark."

A shadow of uncertainty passed across Packard's face. When he didn't respond, Stillman pressed on. "When was this last man killed?"

"Three days ago," Packard said testily. "Not that it has any relevance."

"Hell it doesn't!" Stillman countered. "Three days ago I was in Rock Springs, and I've got witnesses to the fact. You try bringing me to trial and I'll put 'em on the stand. How'd you like to have egg on your face?"

"What were you doing in Rock Springs?"

"That's my business."

"How do I know you're telling the truth?"

Stillman took a chance. "You know because it shows in your face. You're standing there thinking you'd make a fool of yourself if you pressed charges. Am I right or not?"

Packard avoided his gaze. "I hate to admit it, but I agree with you. We've got nothing that would hold up in court."

"Then I'm free to go?"

A quick look passed between Packard and the sheriff. Finally, Packard nodded. "Some people won't understand our letting you loose. I suggest you watch your step."

"I always do," Stillman said. "Sheriff, I'll thank you for my gun."

Hubbard yanked a drawer open and dropped Stillman's gun belt on top of the desk. His features were set in a bearish frown. "Pay close attention," he said. "I'm gonna have a deputy on your ass day and night. Don't even think about leavin' town."

"Sheriff, I wouldn't leave if you ordered me out. I've got unfinished business here."

Stillman left them to ponder his remark. He strapped on his gun belt and moved through the door. On the street, it suddenly occurred to him that he'd been in jail all day. The sun was dipping westward, beyond the mountains, as dusk slowly settled over Tenbow. He walked off toward the hotel.

A few minutes later he entered the lobby. Tom Wexler, who was standing behind the clerk's desk, looked at him with a thunderstruck expression. He crossed to the desk and planted his hands on the counter. His eyes were cold and menacing.

"You sorry sonovabitch," he said. "You sicced the sheriff on me. Told him I was back in town, didn't you?"

Wexler swallowed hard. "How'd you get out of jail?"

"Hubbard and the county prosecutor turned me loose. I convinced 'em they had the wrong man. Any idea who they ought to arrest?"

"How would I know a thing like that?"

Stillman's hand shot out. He took Wexler by the throat and brought him up on his toes. "You remember what you told me about Monty Johnson? That you saw him come out of the saloon just after Judge Taggart was shot?"

Wexler gasped for air, unable to speak. His eyes teared and he nodded his head. Stillman squeezed harder, pulled him halfway across the desk. "Tell me the truth or I'll pop your Adam's apple like an eggshell. You never laid eyes on Johnson that day—did you?"

Wexler's features turned red as oxblood. He

stared back at Stillman with tears streaming down his cheeks. As though summoning his last ounce of strength, he wagged his head from side to side.

"What's that mean?" Stillman said. "Did you or didn't you?"

Wexler gagged a sound, his eyes now blood-shot. Stillman released him and he fell across the desk. His mouth opened, gulping air, and his hands went to his throat. The color slowly returned to his face and his strangled grunts gradually subsided. He recovered sufficiently to push himself off the desk.

"Let's hear it," Stillman demanded. "Yes or no?"

"I swear to God!" Wexler croaked. "Johnson came out of the saloon. I saw him!"

Stillman debated a moment. He'd throttled men before and they seldom lied to him after-ward. Hard as it was to accept, he had a feeling Wexler was telling the truth. But he wasn't yet certain, and his thoughts turned to the daytime bartender at the Tivoli. He wondered where the man might be found at night.

"We'll leave it at that," he said. "But if I find out you're lying, we'll have ourselves another talk. You get my drift?"

Wexler backed away. "I ought to have you arrested."

"Yeah, you should but you won't. You're in

too deep with Devlin to start shouting for the law."

Wexler flinched as though struck by a blow. Stillman saw the reaction and knew his hunch had been confirmed. Turning away, he crossed the lobby and went through the door. Outside, as he stepped off the veranda, he ran into Carl Richter. The cattleman looked startled.

"Stillman!" he said. "Where'd you come from? I've been looking all over for you."

"What's the matter?"

"Some gambler was arrested for the murders. But I've just heard they released him."

"Tell you a secret," Stillman said, smiling. "I'm the gambler you heard about. Here in town, I'm known as Duke Drummond."

"Why'd they arrest you?" Richter said, thoroughly baffled. "Where'd you get that gold tooth?"

"It's a long story."

Stillman gave him the short version. When he finished, Richter appeared confounded. "Let me get this straight. You've been released, but you're still posing as a gambler. Why not take the sheriff into your confidence?"

"That's all part of the same story."

Stillman quickly related what he'd uncovered in Rock Springs. Devlin's land scheme, he noted, provided the motive for the killings. All that remained was to determine who had pulled the trigger. So far he hadn't found the last piece to the puzzle.

"Judas Priest!" Richter swore. "You're saying Devlin meant to steal the whole valley."

"No two ways about it."

"And you believe this Monty Johnson is the killer?"

Stillman nodded. "All I've got to do is prove it. So far I've drawn a blank."

"Hello there, Duke."

A woman's voice brought Stillman around. He turned to find Jennie Blake behind him on the boardwalk. Her eyes crinkled with a smile.

"You're terrible," she said. "You ran out on me again."

"Jennie, I'm sorry," Stillman apologized. "I had some business that needed tending. Could I talk to you later?"

"Only if you promise to stay out of trouble. I was worried sick when I heard they'd arrested you."

"Well, that's water under the bridge now."

"God, I hope so!" She touched his arm with an intimate squeeze. "I was just on my way to work. Will you come by later?"

"You can bet on it."

Stillman waited as she crossed the street, walking toward the Tivoli. Farther uptown he noted a light in the window of Frank Devlin's office. On the spur of the moment he decided to take a more direct line of action. He turned back to Richter.

"Attractive woman," Richter said. "You seem to have made a lot of friends."

"Not near enough," Stillman commented. "Half the people in town are after my hide."

"So what's your next step?"

"I've decided to brace Devlin. One way or another, I'll make him talk."

Richter looked worried. "You're not thinking of taking the law into your own hands, are you?"

"Not unless Devlin forces me to it."

Stillman left him in front of the hotel. As he angled across the street, his features were set in a hard line. Apart from the murders, he told himself, there was a personal score to settle. Devlin had tried to kill him.

When he entered the office, there was a moment of leaden silence. Devlin looked up from his desk, his expression unreadable. Monty Johnson, who was seated in a chair beside the wall, rose to his feet. Neither of them spoke as Stillman halted before the desk.

"Got some bad news," he said to Devlin. "I met a couple of your old friends down at Rock Springs. Orville Brandt and Art Muller."

Devlin stared at him. "There's nothing illegal about my operation here."

"Last time I checked, murder's a hanging offense."

"What's that supposed to mean?"

"Listen real close," Stillman said, his voice cold. "We can do this the easy way or the hard way. What I want is a written confession."

"Confession?" Devlin parroted. "About what?"

"The seven men you had killed."

"You're crazy!"

"Folks won't think so when they hear about your land scheme. They'll probably hang you on general principle."

Johnson moved a step closer. "You got a big mouth," he said. "How'd you like to wind up in the bone orchard?"

Stillman smiled. "You tried that outside the stable the other night. Has your luck changed?"

"Haul ass or you're a dead man."

"Go ahead, try it."

Johnson stood poised with his hand over his gun. A tomblike silence settled on the office, and they stared at each other for a long moment. Stillman looked somehow eager, a razored smile fixed on his mouth. A light flickered and died in Johnson's eyes. He shook his head.

"Another time," he said. "You'll get yours."

Stillman backhanded him across the mouth. He slammed into the wall, blood spurting from a split lip. Before he could react, Stillman pulled his pistol and thumped him over the head. His eyes rolled and his legs buckled at the knees. He slumped to the floor.

Devlin seemed frozen in his chair. Stillman wagged the pistol in his direction. "Let's go."

"Go where?" Devlin blurted.

"Time for you to have a talk with the sheriff."

"I've got nothing to say."

"C'mon, get moving."

Devlin moved around the desk. Stillman prodded him in the back with the snout of the pistol. Outside, they found Carl Richter waiting on the boardwalk. He fell in beside them and they turned up the street in a tight phalanx. After a few steps Stillman grinned.

"I think I just earned my pay."

THIRTEEN

You're out of your head, Drummond."

"Save your breath."

"I'm telling you, I didn't kill anybody."

Stillman nudged him along. "We know you don't do your own dirty work. Somebody else does it for you."

"That's a lie!" Devlin said hotly. "I had nothing to do with those killings."

"And I suppose Johnson took a shot at me all on his own?"

"All right, I'll admit I told him to watch you. I heard you were asking questions about me around town, and I couldn't risk it. How'd you know about Rock Springs, anyway?"

Stillman gave him a shove. "Quit asking so many questions."

"You've got no right!" Devlin fumed. "Who the hell are you, anyhow? A gambler can't arrest people."

"What do you think?" Stillman said, glancing at Richter. "Should we tell him who I am?"

Richter chuckled. "I'll let you have the pleasure."

"Let's save it till he's played songbird for the sheriff. No need explaining it twice."

"You're satisfied he's our man?"

"Nobody else fits the ticket. He's the only one that stood to gain from those killings."

"What about Johnson?" Richter asked. "Shouldn't we have brought him along?"

Stillman smiled. "A gun barrel across a man's head puts him on ice. We'll send a deputy to get him."

"You're certain he's the killer?"

"No, not exactly certain. There could be a third man, somebody hired to pull the trigger. Devlin's gonna tell us all about it—aren't you, Devlin?"

"Go to hell!" Devlin said bitterly. "Nobody'll ever pin those killings on me."

"A week ago you would've said the same thing about your land-grab scheme. You're a hard man to believe."

"I don't give a damn whether you believe me or not. It's the truth!"

A small crowd was by now trailing them along the street. People were drawn by the sight of Stillman's gun and Devlin's heated protests. At the north end of town, they proceeded up the walkway to the courthouse. Lon Hubbard emerged from the front door as they halted at the bottom of the steps.

"What's all this?" he said. "Drummond, why're you holdin' a gun on Mr. Devlin?"

"Sheriff, I think you're in for a long night. Mr. Devlin's got a story he wants to tell you."

"Arrest him!" Devlin shouted. "He abducted me at the point of a gun. I want him locked up."

Stillman holstered his pistol. "I'm placing him in your custody, Sheriff. The charge is murder."

"That's pure hogwash! I haven't murdered anybody!"

Devlin's plea was cut short. A gunshot split the night, rolling in like muted thunder from the east part of town. Stillman and Richter exchanged a puzzled look that slowly turned to certainty. The report had about it the dull boom of a heavy rifle.

An instant later the shrill scream of a woman echoed across the north end of town. Hubbard took hold of Devlin's arm and rushed off into the darkness. The crowd surged along behind, murmuring nervously among themselves. Stillman and Richter brought up the rear, forgotten now in the rush of excitement.

The woman's screams were like a beacon in the night. Hubbard turned onto a side street, where five houses stood spaced some distance apart. The screams suddenly grew louder in pitch, echoing from the last house on the left at the end of the street. The crowd milled around in the front yard as the sheriff hurried forward, waving Devlin aside at the porch. He drew his gun and barged through the door.

Richter looked stunned. "Good God," he said to Stillman. "That's Sam Packard's house."

"The county prosecutor?"

"Yeah," Richter said. "How'd you know that?"

"He questioned me this afternoon."

Stillman pushed through the crowd. The screams turned to low, agonized moans as he crossed the porch. When he entered the door, he found himself in a central hallway that ran the length of the house. On the left, through broad double doors, was the parlor. To the right was the dining room.

The scene reminded Stillman of a slaughter-house. From the doorway he stood surveying the carnage that moments before had been a family gathered around the dining table. Samuel Packard had been shot in the head, blown sideways out of his chair. A rainbow pattern of brains and gore splattered the wall near the door. On the floor around the body, a bright puddle of blood glistened wetly. The dead man looked as though his head had been cleaved apart.

Across the room, Hubbard knelt beside a woman and a small girl huddled in the corner. The woman was sobbing, the girl clutched to her breast, her gaze fixed on the smeared wall. The girl, whose eyes were filled with terror, stared sightlessly at the corpse of her father. The window on the far wall had imploded, scattering shards of glass across the floor. The plates on the table were filled with food, and the serving dishes were undisturbed. A single drop of blood stained the tablecloth before the dead man's chair.

Stillman quickly reconstructed the shooting in his mind. The Packard family had apparently just sat down to their evening meal. Samuel Packard's chair at the head of the table had been directly opposite the window. The killer had had a perfect shot through the window into a well-lighted room, at what amounted to point-blank range. There were no houses east of the Packard home, and the killer had easily approached in the dark, with no fear of being seen. After the shooting, the killer had escaped with equal ease.

Several things seemed to Stillman out of kilter. In the past, the killer had always struck both during daylight hours and at long range. Nor had any of the previous murders been performed in the presence of the victim's family. To all appearances, the killer had taken care to spare the families from the sight of immediate death. Samuel Packard could have been murdered in the same manner, shot from long range from somewhere outside his home. Yet the killer had deliberately elected to shoot Packard before the eyes of his wife and daughter. That indicated a degree of brutality missing in the other murders. Which meant Packard had been singled out.

There was no question that it was the same killer. The massive head wound indicated a heavy-caliber rifle, doubtless a Sharps. But a question surfaced in Stillman's mind as to the involvement of Frank Devlin. There was no animosity between Devlin and Samuel Packard. Nor was Packard opposed in any manner to Devlin's land speculation. So the question arose as to why Devlin would have him murdered. The killings were the work of a third man, that much was certain. Neither Devlin nor Monty Johnson could have fired that shot tonight. But was the killer working for Devlin?

Some visceral instinct told Stillman he'd been wrong. On the surface, because of the land scheme, Devlin seemed the logical suspect. So he had shoe-horned the evidence to fit what appeared to be a motive for the killings. Yet now, staring at Samuel Packard's body, he was no longer convinced. He wondered if the killings were the work of someone with another motive altogether. Someone with an entirely different reason to kill eight men.

The theory gained support from yet another direction. He recalled that Will Sontag and Jud Holt were themselves conducting a search for the killer. Their reasons were unknown, and their search was a closely guarded secret. But after tonight it made a crazy kind of sense. The killings might very well have nothing to do with land speculation or the struggle for control of Tenbow Valley. Instead, the motive might be something far more ordinary. A personal dispute, or perhaps a matter of revenge.

One of Hubbard's deputies hurried into the room. His face went pale at the sight of the corpse and he silently mouthed a curse. He moved around Stillman, skirting the dining table, and stopped beside the sheriff. He motioned outside.

"We found Monty Johnson in Devlin's office. Somebody pistol-whipped him real bad."

Hubbard nodded. "Where is he now?"

"Walt and me brought him here, soon's we heard about . . . this."

"You tend to Mrs. Packard and the girl. Take 'em to one of the neighbors' houses."

"Devlin's outside, too," the deputy added.

"He says it was Drummond that worked over Johnson."

"Figures," Hubbard said. "Go ahead and take care of Mrs. Packard."

The deputy led the sobbing woman and her daughter out of the room. Hubbard moved around the table, halting beside Stillman. He stared down at the dead man, his jaw muscles knotted in rage. At length he forced himself to look away.

"Let's have it," he said curtly. "What's with you and Devlin?"

Stillman spread his hands in a dismissive gesture. "Way things appear, I might've been wrong. Devlin likely had no part in this."

"Were you just trying to get yourself off the hook? Shift the blame onto Devlin?"

"I'm a private investigator. Carl Richter hired me to look into these murders. The name's Jack Stillman."

Hubbard studied him a moment. "Heard stories about you. They say you work in disguise lots of times. Guess you were just pretendin' to be a gamber."

"All part of the job." Stillman unclipped the gold tooth, held it to the light. "A man in my line of work has to fool people sometimes."

"Well, you damn sure made a fool outta me. I'm gonna wind up lookin' like a horse's ass."

"No harm intended, Sheriff."

Hubbard waved him off. "I wanna see you in my office when I'm done here. Don't make yourself scarce."

"I'll be there," Stillman said. "Got some questions I want to ask, anyhow."

"What sorta questions?"

"Nothing that won't keep till later."

Stillman turned toward the doorway. Hubbard stood there, grinding his teeth like an old bear. Then, unwittingly, his gaze was drawn back to the corpse. He spoke aloud to the silent room:

"Goddammit!"

Uptown, Stillman had supper with Carl Richter. Neither of them displayed much appetite and they picked at their food. While they ate, they discussed the killings, trying to isolate something that linked the victims together. Richter was at a loss, more baffled than ever.

Shortly before nine o'clock, they parted outside the café. Richter had decided to spend the night at the hotel, and they made plans to meet later. Stillman turned north, lost in thought as he moved through the flickering glow of street lamps. At the courthouse he proceeded through the hallway to the sheriff's office. He found Hubbard slumped wearily in a chair.

"How'd it go?" he asked, seating himself in

an empty chair "Anything turn up at Packard's house?"

Hubbard pointed at his desk. A spent cartridge case stood upright, balanced on the wide end. "Searched outside with a lantern," he said. "Found this underneath the dining room window. Sonovabitch ejected the shell before he took off."

Stillman fished a cartridge case from his coat pocket. He stood it on the desk with the other one, an exact match. "Sharps .50," he remarked. "I stumbled across it where George Blackburn was killed. Clean shot at better than four hundred yards."

Hubbard stared at the shells, mystified. "I turned Devlin and Johnson loose. Nothin' to hold 'em on."

"You might make a bunco charge stick."

"Bunco—?"

Stillman started at the beginning. He outlined everything he'd uncovered since accepting the assignment. Included in his briefing was the short stay at Will Sontag's ranch as well as the trip to Rock Springs. He concluded on a sour note.

"Hell of it is, I've come full circle. Devlin was my best prospect for the honors."

"Christ," Hubbard said, shaking his head. "Any chance you missed something?"

"Always a chance," Stillman acknowledged.

"But from what I'm told, Devlin and Packard were on friendly terms. Why have him killed?"

"Beats the livin' daylights out of me. I've been stumped since the whole thing started."

For a moment they sat in glum silence. Then Hubbard glanced up with a scowl. "Why'd you leave me in the dark all this time? Least you could've done was tell me who you were."

"No offense, Sheriff," Stillman said. "I prefer to work alone."

"So where's that got you?"

"Tell you the truth—nowhere."

"Any bright ideas what we do now?"

Stillman looked pensive. "All along I figured it had to do with land rights. Even after the judge was killed, everything pointed to the land. But tonight put the quietus on that."

"Yeah, you're right," Hubbard agreed. "Sam Packard wasn't involved no whichaway with land."

"Well, there's got to be a common denominator here somewhere. Nobody kills eight men without a reason."

"No argument on that score. Any man that kills in cold blood, you damn betcha he's got a motive."

"Let's tally up," Stillman said. "Six of the dead men were farmers and small ranchers. That leaves Judge Taggart and Packard."

Hubbard shrugged. "So what?"

"Where's the link?" Stillman said, wondering aloud. "What do farmers and cowmen have in common with a judge and a county prosecutor?"

"I dunno—"

Hubbard's voice abruptly trailed off. He sat upright in his chair and a look of sudden revelation spread across his features. "Jesus H. Christ," he said softly. "Joe Quinn."

"Who's Joe Quinn."

"Used to live hereabouts," Hubbard said. "Claimed he'd been a mountain man in the old days. When settlers moved into the valley, he started trapping wolves for a living."

"Get to the point," Stillman demanded. "What's he got to do with the murders?"

"Judge Taggart sent him to prison. Sam Packard was the prosecutor at his trail. George Blackburn and them other five that got killed was on the jury."

"Hold on," Stillman said. "There's twelve men on a jury. What about the other six?"

"Some died and some pulled up stakes. Them six were all that's left."

"How about you? Didn't you arrest him?"

"Wasn't sheriff then," Hubbard said. "Bob Wilson was in office when it happened. He died of consumption less'n a year after Quinn went to prison."

"When was that?" Stillman prompted. "The year of the trial?"

"Spring of '73. Five years ago."

"What was the term of his sentence?"

"Five years," Hubbard said with a sheepish look. "Couple of months ago, maybe three, I got word he'd served his time. They'd done released him."

"Damnation!" Stillman said gruffly. "Didn't it ever occur to you that he was behind the killings?"

"Never gave it a thought. How the hell you expect me to figure out a thing like that? Lots of men get let out of prison."

"Yeah, but not from Tenbow."

"Quit layin' it off on me," Hubbard snapped. "Nobody's seen hide or hair of him since his release. Wasn't no reason for me to be suspicious."

"Well, he's back," Stillman said. "With the oldest motive in the world—retribution."

"Guess it all fits, don't it?"

"Way it looks to me, he's killed them off one by one. First the jury, then the judge, and now the prosecutor."

Hubbard frowned. "Maybe he's not done yet. Now that I think on it, there's a couple more."

"Who?"

"Will Sontag and his wife."

Stillman tensed. "What have they got to do with it?"

"Sontag's the one that brought charges. Claimed Joe Quinn tried to rape his wife."

"And she testified at the trial?"

"Oh, hell, yes," Hubbard affirmed. "Swore to it under oath. Wouldn't have been no conviction without her."

"Attempted rape?" Stillman said in a musing voice. "How'd she prove that?"

"Some folks thought she didn't. Her reputation's not what you'd call spotless. 'Course, the only ones she had to convince was the jury."

"So there's a chance Quinn wasn't guilty?"

"Just speakin' for myself," Hubbard allowed, "I always had my doubts."

"Everything dovetails," Stillman said. "Quinn saved Sontag and his wife for last. He wanted them to sweat."

"I reckon we ought to warn 'em."

"No need," Stillman said with a clenched smile. "They've known who it was all along."

"What makes you think that?"

"Why else would Sontag have hired Jud Holt? He wanted Quinn tracked down and killed."

Hubbard grunted. "Doesn't seem to have bothered Quinn overly much."

"I'd say he's having a whale of a time. That's why he's been leaving his calling card."

"Calling card?"

"Sitting right there," Stillman said, motioning to the cartridge cases. "He wanted everybody to know it was just one man. And a helluva rifle shot."

"Jesus," Hubbard said. "You make it sound like he wants to get himself caught."

"Not just yet."

"What d'you mean?"

"Not till he kills Will Sontag."

FOURTEEN

The sky was dark with clouds. A drizzling rain began coming down as Stillman walked back to the hotel. The street was deserted except for horses that stood hitched outside the town's saloons. Up ahead, light spilled from the windows of the Tivoli. He crossed to the opposite side of the street.

Jennie Blake would be disappointed. He'd promised to stop by, but his mind was now absorbed with other things. The case was no longer a puzzle wrapped inside an enigma. The killer had been identified, the motive established. Who did what and why was now clear. All that remained was to catch Joe Quinn.

Stillman never questioned that the job was his alone. He'd been hired to stop a killer, not merely solve a mystery. A part of any assignment was putting himself in harm's way, and he accepted the risk. Had he asked, the sheriff would have probably agreed to join him in the manhunt. But the idea of Lon Hubbard and a squad of deputies tagging along was of no interest. What had to be done was best done by one man.

From the vantage of hindsight, the case now seemed downright simple. He thought perhaps it had been a mistake to keep his identity a secret from the sheriff. Had he revealed himself at the outset, there was a possibility that Hubbard might have awakened sooner. Any one of the leads he'd uncovered might have jiggled the sheriff's memory about Joe Quinn. Given that, there was a probability that one or more of the murdered men could have been saved. But then, hindsight made a wizard out of the plainest simpleton. To dwell on what might have been was a fool's game. What counted was the here and now—the next step.

That presented a daunting problem. Knowing the identity of the killer and catching him were two vastly different things. All the more so when the killer's name was Joe Quinn. According to the sheriff, Quinn had once been a mountain man and later a wolf trapper. Any mountain man, even the least of the breed, was a master of the wilderness. Accustomed to living off the land, dependent on woods lore for survival, such men were more akin to wild creatures than ordinary humans. Which explained how Quinn had so effortlessly stalked and killed his victims. He was a seasoned predator, a meat eater who walked upright.

Stillman had no illusions about the job ahead. He was very much a realist about his work, and he never kidded himself. Over the years he'd developed a bag of tricks when it came to hunting men. A good part of that time had been spent in the wilderness, and he was no slouch at hide-and-seek games where civilized rules counted for nothing. Yet he had never undertaken a chase where the man he sought was as wily as Joe Quinn. Worse, he knew beforehand that the game would be played out on Quinn's territory, somewhere within the mountains. To win, merely to emerge alive, he would need all the skill he possessed. And an extra ration of luck.

A single lamp burned in the hotel lobby. Upstairs, he started toward his room, then remembered that Richter was staying the night. He reversed directions and rapped on a door at the end of the hall. Footsteps sounded from within.

"Who's there?"

"Stillman."

A key turned in the lock. Richter opened the door and waved him inside. "Wondered when you'd get back. I was having a helluva time staying awake."

"Won't keep you long," Stillman said. "Just thought I'd bring you up to date."

"What happened with the sheriff?"

"Lots more than I expected."

Stillman recounted everything he'd learned. At the mention of Joe Quinn, Richter's brow furrowed in recognition. By the time he finished, the cattleman appeared dumbstruck. They stared at each other in a moment of profound silence.

"I'll be damned," Richter said finally. "Hubbard must have his head screwed on backward. Why didn't he tell someone Quinn had been released?"

"Not important now," Stillman said. "I know who I'm after and that's all that counts. Tomorrow we start fresh."

"Question is, where do you start?"

"Will Sontag's ranch."

"Why, sure," Richter said, nodding. "Sontag's the bait, isn't he? Quinn's certain to show."

"Maybe, maybe not," Stillman said. "Quinn likes to pick his spot. He might waylay Sontag somewhere besides the ranch."

"So what will you do?"

"For openers, I stake out the house. If nothing happens there, I'll trail Sontag everywhere he goes. Sooner or later, Quinn will punch his ticket."

Richter looked troubled. "Are you saying the only way to find Quinn is to let him kill Sontag?"

"Yeah, more than likely," Stillman said heavily. "I'm not exactly keen on the idea myself. But Quinn never shows till he's ready to make a kill."

"What about Jud Holt?"

"What about him?"

"Well, two sets of eyes are better than one. Maybe you could work together on it."

"No, thanks," Stillman said. "Holt doesn't know beans from buckshot about tracking. I'll go it alone."

Richter was quiet a moment. "I know Quinn from the old days. He was the best wolf trapper in the whole valley. Nobody could hold a candle to him."

"I get the feeling you're trying to tell me something."

"Watch yourself real close, Jack. Quinn's lived in the mountains since long before I met him. He could trap you easy as he used to trap wolves."

"I appreciate the advice," Stillman said. "I'll keep my nose to the wind."

"Just remember, he's already killed eight men. One more wouldn't matter."

"Well, number nine's liable to be Sontag, not me. But that raises a question I wanted to ask you."

"Fire away."

"Sontag knew it was Quinn," Stillman observed. "Way things stack up, he knew it all along. Why didn't he go to the sheriff?"

"Got no idea," Richter said. "But I'll hazard a pretty fair guess. Amanda would fork anything that wears pants. I always suspected she wrongly accused Quinn."

"And?"

"Sontag's the one that forced the issue, not Amanda. He put Quinn in prison, and any fault falls on him. So it's a matter of who gets who first—him or Quinn."

"Yeah, I can see how he wouldn't put much faith in Lon Hubbard."

"Not under the circumstances." Richter paused, his look inquisitive. "When do you aim to leave?"

"Tonight," Stillman said. "I plan to have Sontag's house staked out by daylight."

"What's the rush? Quinn won't show up there this soon. Not after he just killed Packard."

"I never second-guess a man. Especially one with a taste for blood."

"You'd do better to get yourself some sleep. You want a clear head when you go after Joe Quinn."

"Well, like they say, no rest for the weary."

Stillman smiled, turning toward the door. He let himself out and proceeded along the hall to his room. Once inside, he took off his gambler's outfit and hung it in the wardrobe. Then he changed into trail clothes, strapping the Colt to his hip. As he reached for the Winchester and his saddlebags, a knock sounded at the door. He wondered what Richter had forgotten to tell him.

When he opened the door, he found Jennie Blake standing in the hall. Before he could say anything, she smiled brightly and moved past him into the room. He closed the door as she turned to face him.

"Gracious, sugar," she said. "You don't leave a girl any pride."

"Jennie, I meant to stop by—"

"But you're leaving town again, aren't you?"

"How'd you know?"

"Well, for one thing," she said, "we close at midnight. When you hadn't shown up, I got the hint."

Stillman accepted the rebuke. "You have to understand, business comes first. No way I can avoid it."

"I see you have your traveling clothes on. Does that mean you're leaving tonight?"

"Duty calls." Stillman tried a lame smile. "I should've been gone long before now."

She moved closer, placed her arms around his neck. Her breasts were tight against his chest and she kissed him full on the mouth. "You haven't forgotten last time, have you? Up in my room?"

"I'm not likely to forget that."

"Then stay a little while. An hour or so won't matter."

"Wish I could," Stillman said, all too aware of her closeness. "We'll have to save it for another time."

She gave him a pouting look. "You're a great one for promises—that you don't keep."

"Give you my word, I'll keep this one."

She trailed a finger down his cheek, then stepped away. "When will you get back?"

"A day or so," Stillman said. "Depends on how things work out."

"I don't know whether to believe you or not. You've played me for a sucker up till now."

"How's that again?"

"Don't act innocent," she said lightly. "The word's all over town about you—Mr. Stillman."

Stillman wasn't surprised. "Lon Hubbard didn't waste any time, did he?"

"Him and his deputies both! Why, honey, you'd think their pants were on fire. The whole town knows."

"All the more reason I have to leave tonight. I should've figured he'd spread the news."

"You'll take care of yourself . . . for me?"

"No need to worry on that score."

"Just you remember, we've got some unfinished business of our own."

She took his face in her hands and gave him a moist, lingering kiss. Then she vamped him with a sultry look and swept out the door. He stood there a moment, the taste of her still on his mouth. She was one more reason to put an end to the assignment.

He had a promise to keep.

The rain slacked off shortly before dawn. By first light the steady drizzle ended and the sky began to clear. Toward the east the faint blush of sunrise tinged the horizon. There was a crisp bite in the mountain air.

On the wagon road, the rutted tracks were deep with mud. Stillman reined his horse off the road a mile or so before the ranch compound. He'd made poor time, slowed by the combination of rain-soaked ground and pitch-black night. The choice was to get there in one piece or risk taking a spill on the bay. He had held the gelding to a sedate walk.

The last mile seemed to take forever. His approach was through timberland that rose in elevation from the road. Skirting boulders and tangled brush, he gradually made his way toward a wooded ridge. From the time he'd spent at the Lazy S, he remembered a hillside that overlooked the ranch headquarters. The crest would provide a vantage point looking westward, out across the compound and the North Fork of the Popo Agie. He planned to start his surveillance of Sontag from there.

The first rays of sunlight filtered through the woods as he halted on the reverse slope. He stepped out of the saddle and tied the reins to a stout branch on a tree. As he turned away, the rolling boom of a heavy rifle thundered through the mountains. He stood stock still for an instant, filled with a dread awareness of what the gunshot meant. Then he took off running.

Not a minute later he topped the crest of the ridge. Spread out before him were the Lazy S headquarters and the westward mountains. He stopped, breathing heavily from the uphill run, and stared down at the compound. Outside the main corral, he saw the cowhands and a woman gathered around a man sprawled on the ground. There was no question in his mind as to the identity of the fallen man. Will Sontag was dead.

Looking westward, he scanned the forested slopes beyond the compound. Somewhere out there he knew that Joe Quinn had selected a position with a field of fire into the compound. He slowly searched the tree-line along the high ground bounding the river. Instinct told him that he was too late, but he nonetheless hoped to spot movement. To trail the killer, he needed a starting point, fresh tracks. Even as his gaze swept back and forth, he knew he'd fallen a step behind. Joe Quinn was already gone.

One final look was enough. He hurried back to his horse, jerking the reins loose, and mounted. After backtracking a short distance, he swung around the southern base of the ridge. Farther on, through the trees, he emerged onto the road. He nudged the bay into a mud-splattered lope.

Some moments later he rode into the compound. Several of the cowhands, followed by Amanda Sontag, were carrying the rancher's body toward the main house. The others milled around outside the corral, talking in low tones. As Stillman brought his horse to a halt, Slim Bohannon walked forward. He bobbed his head with a doleful expression.

"You missed the fireworks," he said. "The boss just got himself killed."

"I heard the shot up the road a ways. How'd it happen?"

"Him and the boys were gettin' ready to ride out. Next thing you know, somebody drilled him dead center."

Stillman nodded. "Anybody see where the shot came from?"

"Matter of fact," Slim said, "I was standin' over by the bunkhouse. A hawk caught my eye and I happened to lookin' off there."

Slim pointed to a craggy hillside some distance upriver. "Look about halfway up," he said, "where that outcrop splits the aspens. Saw the gunsmoke before I heard the shot."

"Four hundred yards, maybe more," Stillman said, staring at the hillside. "Just like the others."

"Damned if it ain't." Slim paused, scrutinizing him with a puzzled frown. "What brings you back here, anyways?"

"Personal business."

Their attention was drawn to the main house. The hands who had borne Sontag's body trooped out, their faces solemn. As they walked away, Amanda Sontag appeared in the doorway, then stepped onto the porch. Stillman nodded to Slim and rode across the compound. He reined up before the house, noting that the new widow was dry-eyed and seemingly composed. He tipped his hat.

"Sorry about your husband."

"What do you want?" she said. "I thought we'd seen the last of you."

"I'm after Joe Quinn," Stillman said. "You knew it was him all along, didn't you?"

Her face turned ugly. "Who are you?"

"The name's Jack Stillman. I was hired by Carl Richter."

"You're a bounty hunter?"

"Private investigator," Stillman corrected her. "Richter hired me to stop the killings."

She looked at him strangely. "How did you find out about Quinn?"

"The sheriff and I put it together late last night. Sam Packard's death was the tip-off."

"I'm sorry about Packard—and the others."

"'Sorry' won't help," Stillman said flatly. "You should've come to the sheriff when the killings started. If you had, your husband might still be alive."

"I couldn't," she said. "Will wouldn't let me."

Stillman tried a bluff. "Yeah, I can understand that. Guess he didn't want folks to know you'd railroaded an innocent man."

Her reaction confirmed his hunch. A tremor touched her mouth and her eyes misted. "Will was a hard man," she said. "He caught me fooling around with Quinn and he went crazy. After he brought charges, I had to testify the way he told me. I just couldn't humiliate him in public."

"That's a helluva story," Stillman said gruffly. "Eight men died so your husband could save face. Was it worth it?"

She pulled a hankie, dabbed at her eyes. "That's why he hired Jud Holt. He wanted to put things right."

"No, ma'am," Stillman said. "What he

wanted was to get Quinn before Quinn got him. All he cared about was himself."

There was a moment of stiff silence. When she failed to respond, Stillman went on, "Guess that's water under the bridge now. Where's Holt?"

"Gone," she said. "He rode out a few minutes after Will was—"

"Rode out?" Stillman repeated. "Are you saying, he's trailin' Quinn?"

"Yes," she said, suddenly defiant. "What's wrong with that?"

"Goddamn near everything."

Stillman reined his horse around. He gigged the bay with his bootheels and rode off at a lope. Amanda Sontag watched until he forded the river, then turned back into the house. She was no longer thinking of her dead husband or Joe Quinn. She was thinking instead of herself.

How she'd caused the deaths of eight men.

FIFTEEN

The ground was soft from a night's rain. Stillman dismounted where the outcropping of rocks broke the tree line. Ahead, he saw that Holt had been there only minutes before. Horse hooves had left the earth freshly disturbed.

Deliberate now, he walked uphill at a slow pace. He read the sign at a glance and cursed under his breath. The wet ground was churned with horse tracks, a crisscross pattern on either side of the outcrop. A mental image came to him of Holt conducting the search on horseback rather than on foot. He marveled at the man's poverty of skill.

On the north side of the outcrop, he found the spot. Even Holt had found it, though he hadn't paused long. The sign indicated that Joe Quinn had seated himself under an aspen, heels dug into the ground, and taken a solid firing position. After touching off the shot, he'd ejected the spent cartridge, leaving yet another calling card. A brass shell casing glinted in the early morning sun.

Quinn's every movement was clear. He had approached from the reverse slope, walking downhill. Then he'd selected a spot with a clear field of fire into the compound. Since he knew Sontag's morning routine, indications were that he had scouted the position sometime in the past. After killing the rancher, he'd walked up-hill and disappeared over the crest. Imprints of his footsteps were recorded in the damp earth.

Stillman wondered about that. He recalled that Quinn was cautious to the extreme, careful to leave no mark of his passage. All the previous killings had taken place during dry weather, with only sparse sign left in the aftermath. Yet today, with the ground soaked, Quinn had gone ahead with his plans. He could have waited a day, allowed the sun to bake the earth hard. Instead he'd left tracks anyone could read.

To all appearances, Quinn was no longer worried about Jud Holt. Over the past couple of months he had played cat and mouse with Holt throughout the mountains. At the same time, while he had been killing the others involved one by one, he'd let Will Sontag sweat. Clearly, he was saving Sontag until last and wanted Sontag to know it. But with everyone else dead, he couldn't risk Sontag making a run for safety. Which explained why he'd killed Sam Packard last night and then ridden directly to the Lazy S. He meant to end it here today with a final shot, reserved for the man who had sent him to prison. A slug earmarked with Sontag's name.

One last question was removed by today's killing. Quinn was a marksman of the highest order and bold beyond reckoning. He could have shot Sontag and then waited for the rancher's wife to come running out of the house. To reload and fire another shot would have presented no problem whatsoever. All in a matter of seconds Amanda Sontag would have joined her husband in death. Yet it was abundantly clear that Quinn had chosen not to kill the woman. Perhaps he'd known that her husband forced her to give false testimony. Or perhaps there was some lingering sentiment for the woman herself. Either way it spoke well of Joe Quinn.

Downhill, Stillman caught the bay and mounted. He followed the tracks to the crest, pausing a moment on the reverse slope. There he found the tree where Quinn had tied his horse sometime before dawn. The prints were deep and clear in the soft earth, and he studied them at length. He noted that the metal shoe on the right forefoot had a chip in the rounded front edge. From old habit he stared at the print until he'd memorized every detail. Wherever it led, he would know it was Joe Quinn's horse.

The area was muddied as well with the hoofprints of Holt's mount. These were larger and wider, easily distinguished from those of the horse ridden by Quinn. The tracks angled off downhill for a short way before turning westward. From there the trail marched in a straight line toward the distant peaks of the Wind River range. Even Jud Holt could follow such a plain trail, and the hoofprints of his horse indicated he'd moved out at some speed. Oddly, there was no evidence that Quinn had tried to cover his tracks or evade pursuit. He apparently had no fear of being overtaken by the likes of Holt.

Stillman tracked both men throughout the morning. The trail led ever westward, deeper into the mountains. By noontime, the hot midday sun began to dry out terrain situated on open ground. But the land shaded by trees was still damp, and the tracks were plainly visible. Then, as the sun reached its zenith, Stillman suddenly reined to a halt. He stared down at a patch of ground slightly beyond the wooded shoulder of a hill. He saw that Quinn had stopped, turning his horse, and sat watching the backtrail. He saw as well that Quinn would have spotted Holt some distance through the trees. But then, inexplicably, the hunted man had reined about and ridden off.

The sign told a tale in itself. Quinn obviously assumed he was being followed, and he'd stopped to check his backtrail. No less clear was the fact that he could have killed Jud Holt. From where he had stopped, it would have been a simple shot through scattered openings in the woods. Yet he'd passed on the shot, which meant he had no intention of killing Holt. The implications of that one act seemed as plain as the muddy hoofprints. Joe Quinn had killed nine men, all of them responsible in some fashion for his imprisonment. To his twisted way of thinking, the score was now settled in Tenbow Valley. He was ready to call it quits, let the killing end.

Throughout the afternoon, the terrain gradually steepened. The farther west the trail led, the higher it ascended into the mountains. Stillman was now certain of what he'd only suspected before. Somewhere in the remote fastness of the Wind River range, Joe Quinn had established a base camp. A former trapper and mountain man, he would have no trouble living off the land. With little more than coffee beans and cooking gear, he could fare quite well on what the land provided. Operating from the base camp, he had roamed the valley like a phantom on horseback. Then, after every killing, he had simply vanished into the wilderness. Today, quite clearly, he meant to vanish forever.

Late that afternoon, Stillman again reined to an abrupt halt. Before him lay a stretch of rocky terrain bordering a stream. Not far ahead he spotted sign where Quinn had crossed the stream onto soft ground along the opposite bank. A short distance beyond that point the sun had baked the upper shoreline as hard as brick. There, as though his horse had taken wings, Quinn's tracks disappeared. Holt's tracks, on the other hand, indicated that he'd ridden back and forth, searching for the lost trail. Finally, assuming he would cut sign farther on, he had ridden upstream. And never a thought that he'd been hoodwinked.

The trick was old but cleverly done. Stillman dismounted, then turned back, and proceeded downstream. He stuck to the rocky terrain, moving along at a slow walk. Through the clear water he saw small stones overturned within the streambed, their unwashed sides now facing upward. A short distance downstream he found a scuff mark, metal on stone, where Quinn had reined his horse from the creek onto the rocky shoreline. Beyond, where trees bordered the bank, he spotted the faint imprint of a horseshoe. The trail led north through the timber.

Stillman stood there for a long while. At some point he had expected that Quinn would throw Jud Holt off the trail. So that came as no

surprise, and Holt would now spend an uncomfortable night in the mountains. What unsettled him was that Quinn had backtracked so
far downstream. Not ten feet from where he
stood, on soft ground below the rocky stretch,
he saw the tracks of his own horse headed upstream. From the sign he saw that he'd ridden
past only moments after Quinn had quit the
stream and taken to the timber. Which meant
he had to assume that Quinn had seen him.
That Quinn knew someone else was following
the trail.

Standing there, Stillman realized he'd lost
the edge. Having ditched Holt, Quinn would
have normally relaxed his guard. From that
point, tracking him would have been a relatively simple matter. But he'd now been alerted
to a second threat, another man only a short
distance behind. There was no doubt he would
watch his backtrail, once again turn cautious,
and attempt evasive maneuvers. Should all that
fail, he might do something more, something to
ensure his escape. He might decide to make it
ten dead men.

Off to the west, the sun dropped slowly beyond the spires of the mountain range. Stillman saw that he would have no choice but to
make a cold camp. A fire would light the night
like a beacon, and perhaps prove too tempting
for Quinn to resist. He unsaddled and picketed

the bay within the tree line. There was water to drink and he'd noticed a bearberry bush near the creek. While it was short rations, he decided it was supper enough for the night. Tomorrow he'd think about something more filling.

As dusk settled over the land, he unwrapped his bedroll. He sat down on the blanket, munching a handful of berries, and stared off into the woods. His thoughts were on tomorrow, what lay ahead. The trail he was bound to follow.

He wondered where Quinn would be waiting.

Stars faded from the sky as night turned to false dawn. Stillman awoke in the dusky light, wrapped in his blanket. He lay without moving for a minute or longer, listening intently. When a man stepped from his bedroll not yet fully alert, he was most vulnerable. A crafty killer would approach the camp under cover of darkness and wait for first light. His victim, groggy with sleep and clearly visible, made an easy shot.

From the woods Stillman heard the rustle of birds flitting through the trees. There was no absence of sound, which usually indicated that wild things had sensed a foreign presence. He walked to the stream and briskly scrubbed his face. Then he hobbled the gelding and let it forage on the sparse graze along the bank. Afterward, he made breakfast on bearberries and cold mountain water. He waited until full light to saddle the bay.

Long ago he'd learned that a wilderness manhunt required patience. A seasoned tracker always awaited sunrise before trying to cut sign. On hard ground the correct sun angle often made the difference between seeing a print or missing it entirely. The tracker stationed himself so that the trail would appear directly between his position and the sun. In early morning, with the sun at a low angle, he worked westward of the trail. The easterly sunlight would then cast shadows across the faint imprints of man or horse.

A tracker seldom saw an entire footprint or hoofprint unless the ground was quite soft. On rocky terrain there was even less likelihood that complete prints would be spotted. What the tracker looked for instead were flat spots, scuff marks, and disturbed vegetation. Of all sign, flat spots were the most revealing. Only hooves or footprints, something related to man, would leave flat spots. Small creatures might leave faint scuff marks or disturb pebbles. But a flat spot, unnatural to nature, was always made by a hooved animal or a man.

Leading the bay, Stillman moved off on foot

through the timber. The trail he followed was now roughly twelve hours old but still faintly visible. He kept the sun between himself and the hoofprints, which moved uphill in a straight line. Below the crest he found a spot where Quinn had stopped yesterday at dusk, watching his backtrail. The tracks then moved on across the crest, angling off in a northwesterly direction. Yet there was no doubt that Quinn knew he was being dogged by a second tracker. From where he'd paused, he would have had a clear view of the stream downhill. He had probably watched Stillman camp for the night.

A mile or so farther along the trail Quinn had halted, probably as full dark settled over the mountains. Stillman found where he'd made a cold camp and slept the night. The impress of his body and threads from a wool blanket were visible on the ground. Between two trees, where he'd picketed his mount, the imprint of a chipped horseshoe was stamped into the earth. A pile of horse droppings was dark and crusted, but still soft inside when punched with a stick. Only a few flies buzzed the droppings, and that was the best indication of age. The older the droppings, the fewer the flies.

Stillman estimated that Quinn had moved out at first light. As he inspected the tracks leading from the campsite, he looked for the change of color caused by the dry surface of the earth having been disturbed to expose a moister, lower surface. Heat increased the rate at which tracks age, and the sun had been out now for more than an hour. The under surface of the hoofprints was almost restored to the normal color of the ground. All the signs indicated that he was slightly more than two hours behind Quinn.

The trail moved generally west by north, ever deeper into the mountains. Yet the tracks took on an irregular zigzag pattern through canyons and streams and forested slopes. Quinn clearly knew he was being pursued, and he'd resorted to evasive tactics. Wherever possible, he chose rocky terrain or ground baked hard as flint from the summer sun. His general direction never deviated, which meant that his hideout was somewhere in the northern stretch of the Wind River range. But he was taking the long way around in an effort to throw off pursuit.

By midday, Stillman had covered better than ten miles. The tracking was slow and tedious, for he found himself pitted against a veteran of wilderness survival. A good part of the time he was forced to dismount and conduct the search on foot. At several points, particularly on hard ground, the hoofprints simply disappeared. He then had to rely on pebbles and twigs embed-

ded in the earth's surface during past periods
of rain. The number of pebbles and twigs dis-
lodged indicated a hooved animal had passed
that way. The direction in which they moved,
invisible except to a skilled tracker, indicated
the line of travel. Slowly, sometimes step by
step, he clung to the trail.

Shortly after noonday he came upon a trou-
bling sign. On a streambed deep in a canyon,
he discovered that Quinn had again stopped to
watch his backtrail. The spot was located at a
bend in the stream where massive boulders
butted up against the canyon wall. Hidden behind the boulders, Quinn had dismounted and
waited, with a clear view of almost a mile
downstream. From there he could have ended
the chase with an easy shot from his Sharps rifle. Yet he had elected not to kill his pursuer; instead he'd redoubled his evasive maneuvers.
Once more it indicated a reluctance to kill anyone not directly involved with sending him to
prison.

Stillman was nonetheless uneasy. The longer
he stuck to the trail, the more certain it became
that Quinn would be unable to lose him. At
some point Quinn would arrive at the same
conclusion, or he might simply tire of the cat-
and-mouse game. Either way, his reluctance to
kill a stranger might cease to be a factor. All the
more so since the gap separating them had

now been shortened to less than an hour. But the risk was outweighed in Stillman's mind by a sense of challenge and his bulldog determination. He'd never quit before a job was done.

Late that afternoon he topped a wooded ridge. Before him the terrain dropped off and then rose steeply to another ridge perhaps a quarter mile away. The sun had heeled over to the west and the landscape was bathed in fiery brilliance. From the opposite ridge, he caught the flicker of sunlight on metal, winking at him through a stand of trees. Operating on instinct, certain that he was framed in Quinn's gun sights, he rolled sideways out of the saddle. A puff of smoke billowed from the distant tree line.

Stillman never heard the shot. When he was halfway out of the saddle, a slug plowed into his left side and deflected off his rib cage. The impact lifted him clear of the saddle and dropped him heavily on the ground. His last thought before the world went dark was that he'd pressed too hard.

Joe Quinn had decided to end the game.

SIXTEEN

The bay gelding stood swishing flies with its tail. Off to the west the lowering sun touched the tallest peaks of the Wind Rivers. Somewhere in the distance a bluejay pierced the silence of the mountains.

Stillman lay where he'd fallen. He was motionless, sprawled on his back, his eyes closed. His hat was upended beside him and his hair seemed sprinkled with fire from the setting sun. Flies buzzed the welter of blood seeping through the left side of his shirt.

The scolding cry of the bluejay sounded closer. Stillman's eyes fluttered open and he lay staring at the sky. His vision was blurred and even the dome of the sky seemed oddly out of focus. Then he blinked, lowering his eyes, and slowly made out the trunk of a nearby tree. As his vision cleared, he became aware that he was lying on the ground. He remembered throwing himself out of the saddle.

Sudden pain stabbed through his side. He groaned, wincing at the fire that spread across his rib cage, and his forehead beaded with sweat. His hand went to his side and came away wet with blood. He remembered then, recalling that last instant when he'd seen the flash of sunlight on metal from the opposite ridge. Afterward, there was a void of recollection, an abrupt lapse into darkness without memory. He realized now that he'd been shot.

Some moments passed before he tried to move. Finally, with his right hand braced against the ground, he levered himself upright. The pain lanced through his entire left side, so sharp that it took his breath. A woozy sensation clouded his vision and he thought he might fall backward. But he steadied himself, holding on until the dizziness gradually faded away. At last, gritting his teeth against the pain, he shifted around with his back to the tree trunk. He took several shallow breaths, waiting while the pain eased off to a dull throb. Then he began exploring the wound.

Working slowly, he pulled his shirttail out. He lifted it high on his chest, pushing his leather vest aside, and clamped it in place with his left hand. By bending slightly at the waist, he was able to lower his head and see the

wound. The slug had entered at the top of his
rib cage, then deflected off the bone on a downward angle. His side was laid open to the belt
line, where the slug had exited at waist level.
The bloody furrow was nasty-looking but not
as bad as he'd feared. So far as he could determine by touch, only one rib had been cracked.

A split second in time was all that had saved
him. By throwing himself out of the saddle, he
had taken the slug in the ribs rather than
through the chest. The wound was by no means
mortal, but he'd been badly hurt. Loss of blood
and infection were his most immediate con-
cerns. Somehow he had to stanch the flow of
blood before his condition weakened any further. At the same time he had to cleanse the
wound to ward off the risk of infection. Over the
years he'd seen men die not from the gunshot itself, but rather the infection that invaded their
bodies. The process was slow and agonizing, a
hard death. He meant to live awhile longer.

The ridge dropped off into a wooden
canyon. Far below he saw sunlight sparkling
off a fast-running mountain stream. The trick
was to get there in one piece, without further
aggravating his wound. He steeled himself
against the pain, bracing his back with the tree,
and pushed to his feet. After pulling his shirt
down, he snugged it against his side with his
left arm, slowing the bleeding. He hobbled to-

ward his horse, thankful that the bay was not skittish by nature. One foot in the stirrup, he grabbed the saddle horn with his right hand and swung aboard. A hot, knifelike sensation seared his ribs.

When he'd collected himself, he nudged the bay over the forward slope. The ride downhill was slow and torturous, every jounce and jostle sending waves of pain ripping through his side. At the bottom of the slope he reined into a small clearing surrounded by trees. Gripping the saddle horn, he lowered himself to the ground and stood for a moment to let his head clear. Then he unlashed his bedroll and saddlebags, and dropped them at his feet. As he turned toward the stream, he realized that sunset was less than an hour away. There was no time to waste.

Seated beside the stream, he dug a kerchief from his hip pocket. He let it trail in the shallows, allowing the swift, clear water to rinse it clean. Then, while it was soaking wet, he spread the kerchief over his rib cage. The water cleansed the wound, and the cloth, icy cold from the stream, stemmed the flow of blood. He repeated the process several times, until finally the seepage of blood slowed to a mere trickle. Satisfied, he rinsed the kerchief and wrung it out one last time. He got to his feet, steadier now, feeling stronger.

A short distance into the woods, he found

what he needed. Between two trees a spider had woven a large, intricate web that looked like spun silk. He started with the strands on one side and carefully worked across the web, folding it into a thick, matted compress. When he placed it on his side, the spider web formed an absorbent shield over the wound. For added protection he spread the kerchief and used it to cover the bandage formed by the web. Then, after cutting strips from his blanket, he knotted them around his waist and chest, securing the compress. Within minutes the seepage of blood stopped altogether.

Food was the next order of business. He'd had nothing to eat but berries for the past two days, and even a healthy man need sustenance. With a gunshot wound, what he needed now was red meat, enough to restore his strength. Scouting farther into the woods, he located a game trail used by rabbits. He cut two small stakes with his belt knife and notched both of them at one end. A strip of rawhide from his saddlebags was fashioned into a noose, and the tail end was tied to the top of a springy sapling as well as one of the stakes. The other stake was driven into the ground; when the sapling was bent over, the notches on both stakes joined together to hold it down. The noose was then draped across the center of the game trail, with either side loosely held open by low bushes. A rabbit caught in the noose would cause the notched stakes to release, transforming the sapling into a makeshift gallows.

Dusk had fallen by the time he returned to the clearing. Favoring his left side, he unsaddled the bay, fitted it with hobbles, and turned it loose to graze. Afterward, he found a huckleberry bush ripe with fruit and ate his fill. Sometime during the night, he felt certain, a rabbit would wander into the snare and provide a substantial breakfast. As dusk turned to dark, he gathered brushwood and built a small fire. He spread his bedroll near the fire and stretched out on his back. The warmth of the blaze, combined with the effects of his wound, almost immediately sapped him of energy. His eyelids dropped, and in that last instant before sleep his thoughts went to Joe Quinn. A tight smile creased his mouth.

Quinn had shot him and left him for dead. But instinct, and no small amount of luck, had saved his bacon. Against all odds, he'd lived to fight another day. Tomorrow or the next day, no matter.

Time was nothing to a man left for dead.

A squirrel chattered somewhere in the trees. The sun, like a globe of fire, slowly edged over the horizon. Wrapped in his tattered blanket, Stillman awoke as shafts of light spread across the clearing. His first thought was that he'd survived the night.

Gingerly, moving a part here and a part there, he tested himself. He was sore and he ached, and his entire left side felt as though he'd been whopped with a sledgehammer. But the searing pain had diminished to a dull, constant throb. The spiderweb bandage was plastered tightly over his wound, and there was no sign of fresh bleeding. All things considered, he felt like he'd come through in good shape.

As he stepped from the bedroll, his stomach grumbled. He realized that he was famished, and his thoughts went immediately to the snare. A tendril of smoke drifted from the burned-out campfire, and downstream he saw the bay grazing on a patch of grass. Somewhat stiff, still favoring his left side, he walked off into the woods. On the same trail he saw a fat rabbit dangling from the sprung sapling. His stomach rumbled louder as he slipped the noose free.

After rekindling the fire, he dressed the rabbit and washed it in the stream. The carcass was then spitted on green branches and set to roast over low flames. While he waited, he gathered a handful of berries and took a seat on his bedroll. As he munched, he considered his situation in the light of a new day. His wound was serious, and by all rights he should remain camped until the healing process was underway. Yet he'd always been quick to recover from injury, and his tolerance for pain was unusually high. So long as the wound wasn't reopened, he saw no reason not to travel. He could abide discomfort far easier than idleness.

For that matter, tracking his man would now be considerably simpler. Joe Quinn thought he was dead, buzzard bait left to rot in the summer sun. With all pursuit eliminated, Quinn would no longer resort to evasive tactics. Instead there was every likelihood that he'd made a beeline for his base camp. The shortest route was often the easiest route, especially when there was no reason to lay a false trail. That made tracking not only simpler but a whole lot faster. A man who believed himself safe from pursuit always left plenty of sign. Quinn would prove to be no exception.

When the rabbit was cooked, Stillman tore into it like a ravenous wolf. He started at the front and worked his way back, stripping every last shred of meat from the bones. Though his hunger was by no means slaked, he decided to save one of the hindquarters. He figured Quinn's camp was somewhere close by, less than a day's ride away. But he couldn't be certain, and if he had to spend another night on the trail, the hindquarter would make a welcome supper. He wrapped it in an extra pair of socks from his saddlebags.

Ten minutes later he rode across the stream. At the top of the ridge, he found the spot from where Quinn had shot him. The sign from that point onward, just as he'd suspected, was easy to read. He followed on horseback, holding the bay to a steady walk.

The trail led due northwest.

By midday, Stillman was deep in the Wind River range. The terrain steepened gradually, heavily forested along the slopes. Beyond the timberline the mountains towered higher than thirteen thousand feet. The spires were framed by silverwhite clouds that hung motionless in the sky.

All morning the trail had seldom deviated. The sign was straight as a string, due northwest, except for an occasional detour to avoid rough terrain. Quinn knew where he was headed and he'd clearly been in a hurry to get there. No attempt had been made to cover the telltale tracks of his horse. The hoofprint with the chipped shoe was plain to read.

Stillman smelled the smoke before he saw it. High in the mountains, the wind was generally borne along on a downdraft. He reined to a halt, shading his eyes against the overhead sun, and stared at the skyline. Not far ahead he saw a thin plume of smoke rising from a wooded knoll. There was no doubt in his mind that he'd found Joe Quinn. After dismounting, he tied his horse to a tree and pulled the Winchester from his saddle scabbard. Warning himself to caution, he turned uphill.

Stealth was the key to surprise. Unless forced to it, he preferred not to kill Quinn. Far better to take him alive and let the law dispense justice. Since he was downwind, he wasn't worried that Quinn's horse might raise his scent. Yet he'd learned the hard way that Quinn was sly as a fox, never to be underestimated. He moved through the woods a step at a time, pausing to scout ahead. There was no margin for error, for he was hunting a hunter. A mistake now might well be his last.

The ground leveled off onto a wide knoll. Through the trees, perhaps thirty yards away, he saw movement. He froze, every sense alert, watching the figure of a man move about a small clearing. Off to one side a saddle horse and a packhorse were picketed in the woods. The man was solidly built, dressed in buckskins, with shaggy hair and a full beard. He appeared to be breaking camp, gathering gear and stuffing it into packs. Since he had killed all his enemies, there was a certain logic to leaving Tenbow Valley. Quinn was preparing to take off for parts unknown.

Stillman catfooted through the timber. He stopped at the edge of the clearing, partially hidden behind a tree. All in a motion he brought the Winchester to his shoulder and cocked the hammer.

"Don't move!" he ordered. "You're covered."

Quinn was stooped down, lashing the straps on a pack. He was facing in the opposite direction, and at the command from his rear he exploded into action. Hurling himself sideways, he hit the ground rolling and jerked his pistol. He fired a quick snapshot in the same instant Stillman triggered the Winchester. A slug thudded into the tree at Stillman's side, and he saw his own shot kick dirt at Quinn's feet. As he levered a fresh cartridge into the Winchester, Quinn rolled behind the terrified horses and vanished into the woods. There was no time for a second shot.

Stillman muttered a harsh curse. He'd lost the edge by trying to take his man alive. But there was no turning back now, for it was kill or get killed. Quinn wouldn't run far, and he had no choice but to follow. What it boiled down to was hunter against hunter, a deadly contest of hide-and-seek. The next shot fired would likely be the last shot of the fight.

The horses were walleyed with fright, kicking and snorting at their picket line. Stillman kept to the trees, circling around the horses, and halted where Quinn had disappeared. He saw the outline of footprints, clearly visible from the force of a man's running stride. His

eyes darted from the ground to the woods,
sweeping and searching as he moved forward.
Ten yards farther on, the hunt turned to a slow
stalk.

Deep within the tree line, where he was out
of sight, Quinn had stopped running. His
tracks were now faint imprints, discernable
only by close scrutiny of the ground. The trace
of his passage was evident for the most part
from heel marks. On level terrain, even when a
man treads lightly, the heel absorbs the initial
impact of the entire body. The rounded curve of
heel made a distinct print, unlike anything
found in nature. The tracks angled off toward
the west.

A short distance ahead a huge, moss-covered
boulder stood like a monolith in the woods. As
Stillman approached it, he became wary of
what lay on the other side of the boulder. Caution dictated that Quinn was on the other side,
hidden in the woods, waiting for him to move
into view. He paused at the edge of the boulder,
scanning the ground directly ahead. Then, suddenly, the hair on the back of his neck bristled.
He saw heel marks on a straight line extending
past the boulder. But he saw as well the single
imprint of a toe mark overlapping one of the
heel prints. From the look of it, Quinn had
stepped backward into his own tracks.

Stillman flattened himself against the boul-

der, staring upward. His every instinct told
him that Quinn wasn't waiting in the woods
beyond, ready to spring an ambush. Instead
the foxy old mountain man had walked backward in his tracks and scrambled to the top of
the boulder. He was up there even now, flat on
his belly, waiting for Stillman to move into the
clear. Then, at short range, a pistol shot in the
back would end the hunt.

There was nowhere to run, nowhere to hide.
On sudden impulse Stillman squatted down,
took hold of a large rock, and tossed it ahead
into the woods. As the rock struck the ground,
he stepped clear of the boulder and raised the
Winchester. Quinn was framed against the
skyline, rising swiftly to his feet, the pistol extended toward the woods beyond. A shock of
surprise crossed his features, and he tried to
reverse directions, swinging the pistol
around. Stillman shot him in the chest, and he
stood there a moment, his gun arm arrested in
motion. Abruptly, as though his legs failed
him, he tumbled off the boulder and hit the
ground.

Stillman jacked a cartridge into the Winchester. He moved closer, kicking Quinn's pistol
aside, and knelt down. A widening splotch of
blood stained the buckskin shirt and he saw
that it was a mortal wound. Quinn stared up at
him with a strange look.

"Plumb fooled me," he said. "Thought I'd got you back there on that ridge."

"You did," Stillman told him. "Guess it wasn't my day to die."

"What's your name?"

"Does it matter?"

"Just like to know who killed me."

Before Stillman could reply, Quinn's eyes glazed over. A trickle of blood seeped out of his mouth and his head rolled sideways. Stillman stared at him for a long moment, somehow saddened. Under different circumstances they might have shared a campfire, swapped a few lies. But that would never happen now.

Joe Quinn was dead.

SEVENTEEN

Stillman rode into Tenbow late the next afternoon. Trailing behind him on lead ropes were the horses he'd brought down from the mountain camp. Quinn's body was tied across the packhorse.

At first there was little notice of the unusual caravan. Stillman entered town from the north, passing only one wagon on the road. But as he approached the courthouse, several people on the street spotted his grisly cargo. By the time he dismounted, a small crowd had gathered, watching from a distance. He left the horses tied to the hitch rack.

Inside the courthouse, he moved directly to the sheriff's office. Lon Hubbard looked at him as though an apparition had walked through the door. His haggard features, along with the bloodstained shirt, gave him the appearance of a man more dead than alive. He closed the door without a word and dropped wearily into a chair. Hubbard stared across the desk with an awestruck expression.

"You're alive," he said with a dopey smile. "By God, you're actually alive!"

Stillman frowned. "You sound surprised."

"Damn right," Hubbard said. "When I heard you were on Quinn's trail—"

"Who told you that?"

"Jud Holt busted in here with fire coming out of his ears. Wanted to know why I hadn't told him you were on the case."

"Wait a minute," Stillman said. "Are you saying Holt thought we were working together?"

"Well, yeah," Hubbard said lamely. "He just naturally figured you'd cooperate with the law."

"Funny he'd think that. Especially when he never told anybody why Sontag really hired him."

"Holt's not one to offer explanations. But he's some pissed off about you pretendin' to be a bronc buster. Figures you suckered him real good."

"Tough," Stillman grunted. "I don't give a damn what Holt thinks."

"Forget Holt," Hubbard said, suddenly eager. "Tell me about Joe Quinn. What happened?"

"We took turns shooting at each other. I got the last shot."

"You killed him?"

Stillman nodded. "Have a look outside and see for yourself. He's the one draped over a horse."

"Outside?" Hubbard blurted. "How long's he been dead?"

"Little more than a day."

"Christ, he must be gettin' ripe. Why'd you bring him back to town?"

"Without a corpse," Stillman said, "it wouldn't be official. I want a coroner's inquest."

"Inquest?" Hubbard said, astounded. "What the hell for?"

"Way I see it, Joe Quinn got a raw deal. Folks ought to know what really killed him."

"You're talkin' about Sontag and his wife—aren't you?"

"Nobody else."

Hubbard looked troubled. "You haul Miz Sontag into an inquest and Jud Holt's liable to blow his cork. From what I hear, he's taken a shine to her."

"That's his problem," Stillman said. "You go ahead and set up the inquest."

"Guess I've got no choice."

Stillman climbed to his feet. "Who's the best sawbones in town?"

"Doc Phillips," Hubbard noted. "He's also the county coroner. Why'd you ask?"

"Quinn left me with a little souvenir. Thought I'd get some professional advice."

"Way you look, that's not a bad idea."

"Let me know when and where on the inquest."

Stillman walked from the courthouse. After dropping his bay at the livery stable, he got directions to the doctor's office. A few minutes later he was seated on an examining table, stripped to the waist. Doc Phillips, using a damp sponge, slowly loosened the spiderweb bandage. He inspected the wound with clinical curiosity.

"That's rich," he said, chuckling. "A spiderweb! Old-time folk medicine at its best."

"Way it happened," Stillman observed, "I had to use whatever was handy. How's it look?"

"Why, it's coming along fine, Mr. Stillman. All things considered, it's really quite remarkable."

"No infection?"

"None a'tall," Phillips said. "The bruised tissue and all that redness is normal. Of course, you're going to have a rather extraordinary scar. No way to avoid that."

Phillips smeared a medicinal ointment on the wound and covered it with a gauze bandage. He'd already heard about Joe Quinn's death, as had the whole town. When Stillman informed him that an inquest would be ordered, he merely nodded and said nothing. Stillman left the office wondering whether his detached air represented objectivity or indifference. Or perhaps, like so many physicians who also served as coroners, he simply didn't care for inquests. Doctors, for whatever reason, were often uncomfortable discussing death.

Worn out, his step heavy with fatigue, Stillman walked to the hotel. He ignored Tom Wexler, who froze behind the clerk's desk as he crossed the lobby. In his room, he discarded his clothing and took a bird bath in the washbasin. After replacing the water, he lathered his face and shaved a four-day growth of beard. A knock sounded at the door as he stepped into a clean pair of trousers.

"Who's there?"

"It's me, sugar—Jennie."

Stillman slipped into a shirt before he opened the door. Jennie threw herself into his arms and kissed him roundly on the mouth. He winced when she snuggled close against his chest, and stepped back. Her expression went round-eyed with alarm.

"Omigod!" she said. "I heard you'd been wounded, but nobody thought it was real bad. Are you all right, sugar?"

"Just a scratch," Stillman assured her. "Don't worry about it."

"You're sure?" she insisted. "I mean, the way you jumped when I hugged you! That sounds like more than a scratch."

"Give you my word, it's nothing serious."

"Well—" She studied him doubtfully. "To tell you the truth, lover, you look like hell. I think maybe I'll have to nurse you back to health."

Stillman thought her nursing care might finish him off. He gave her a game smile. "What I need is a good night's sleep. Things have kept me hopping the last few days."

"Now don't you be modest, sugar. Everybody knows how you tracked that awful man down and shot him. I think it's wonderful!"

She looked all but ready to pin a medal on him. Stillman was trying to frame a suitable reply when someone rapped on the door. He moved past her, opening the door, and found Carl Richter in the hall. The cattleman grabbed his hand and pumped it, beaming a wide smile.

"By golly, Jack," he said briskly, "you're a sight for sore eyes. I'd about given you up for lost."

"How'd you know I was back?"

"Good news travels fast," Richter said. "I've been staying at the hotel since you left. Went downstairs a minute ago and heard you'd come in."

Stillman nodded. "Then you've probably heard about Quinn?"

"Yeah, I have," Richter said soberly. "'Course, it's just as well things ended that way. Joe Quinn on the gallows would've made a sorry spectacle."

Jennie moved across the room. She flashed Richter a look that told him three was a crowd. But then, smiling brightly, she kissed Stillman on the cheek. "I'm late for work, sugar. Drop by when you're through here."

"All depends," Stillman said. "Once I hit that bed, I'm probably out for the night. You'll like me better after a night's sleep, anyhow."

"I like you any way I can get you, lover."

When she'd gone, Stillman turned back into the room. Richter gave him a wry look. "That little lady has eyes for you, Jack. Better watch your step."

"Guess so," Stillman said, taking a seat on the edge of the bed. "But I wasn't lying to her. I'm about to drop in my tracks."

"Then I'll be quick," Richter said. "There's a couple of things you ought to know about right off. First, Frank Devlin and Monty Johnson have spread the word that you're an out-and-out liar."

"About their land scheme?"

"Exactly," Richter said gravely. "Devlin denies any knowledge of the railroad's plans. To hear him tell it, you'd think he was a prophet. He claims he had a vision about good times ahead in Tenbow Valley."

"Anybody swallow that hogwash?"

"Some folks have no qualms about dealing with the devil. Not when there's enough money involved. Lots of people think Devlin will make them rich."

"Only half rich," Stillman commented. "He'd figure a way to steal the other half."

"I agree," Richter said forcefully. "Devlin's crooked, but he's stayed within the letter of the law. He hasn't actually committed fraud. From a legal standpoint our hands are tied."

Stillman looked at him. "I assume you're telling me all this for a reason. Why not get to it?"

"I want Devlin out of town! The sheriff won't do it, so I'm asking for your help. Tenbow doesn't deserve the likes of Devlin."

"Last time I went after Devlin, you thought I was taking the law into my own hands. What's changed?"

Richter spread his hands. "I suppose I've changed. The law's not effective against men like Devlin. So somebody else . . ." He paused, dropped his hands. "Will you help?"

"All you had to do was ask," Stillman said. "We'll have a talk with Devlin first thing in the morning. You said there were a couple of things I ought to know—?"

"Let's call the second one a warning."

"Warning about what?"

"Jud Holt," Richter advised him. "There's talk that he blames you for Sontag's death. Maybe he's serious, maybe he's not. But you shouldn't take it lightly."

"Appears I'm double warned," Stillman said. "The shcriff told me the same thing when I asked for an inquest into Quinn's death."

"Why would you want an inquest?"

"Joe Quinn deserves his day in court. I aim to see that he gets it."

"Will you force Amanda Sontag to testify?"

Stillman nodded. "You might say she's the key witness for the defense."

"Holt won't like it," Richter said. "You're liable to have trouble with him."

"Far as I'm concerned, he can like it or lump it."

"Well, you sleep on it. Don't do anything rash."

Richter let himself out the door. Stillman fell back on the bed, his eyes starting to close as his head hit the pillow. His last waking thought was of Jud Holt and Amanda Sontag.

He wondered if they'd gotten together before her husband was killed.

• • •

A night's sleep left Stillman refreshed and restored. When he awoke, he stretched the length of the bed, testing himself. His side ached, and the scab over the wound was tender and sore. But that was to be expected, all part of healing. He felt better than he had since the day he was shot.

While he was dressing, his mind turned to Carl Richter. Some men believed in the sanctity of the law, an inviolate code that worked only because it was so rigid. Yet their beliefs were often challenged when the law proved incapable of dealing with a borderline situation. Even the best of men would then look to means that skirted the letter of the law. For Richter that borderline situation was represented by Frank Devlin. He'd decided to bend the rules.

Stillman suddenly realized he was starving. Too worn out to eat, he'd skipped supper last night. But now, as his stomach registered a protest, the thought of breakfast made his mouth water. Out in the hall, he rapped on Richter's door, and they left the hotel together. In the café across the street, they ordered steak and eggs, biscuits with wild honey, and black coffee. While they ate, there was no mention of Devlin or how the situation would be handled. Richter seemed content not to press the issue.

Outside, Stillman paused to light a cheroot.

Then, with Richter at his side, he walked directly to Devlin's office. When they came through the door, Devlin remained seated behind his desk. Monty Johnson, who was cleaning his fingernails with a pocketknife, got to his feet and backed against the wall. He closed the knife and shoved it into his pants, watching Stillman with a hard scowl.

"Good morning," Devlin said with feigned pleasantry. "And in your case, Mr. Stillman, I understand congratulations are in order. Yessir, you've made Tenbow safe again."

"Cut the crap," Stillman said bluntly. "I'm here to talk business."

"What sort of business?"

"How and when you're gonna leave town."

Devlin laughed. "What makes you think I'm leaving town?"

"Way I see it," Stillman said, "you've got two choices. First, I could walk back to the hotel and lean on Tom Wexler. We both know he'd spill his guts."

"About what?" Devlin said with a dismissive gesture. "I have no connection with Wexler."

"Yeah, you do," Stillman countered. "Wexler's a silent partner in your land-grab scheme."

"That's too farfetched for belief. Nobody would listen to you."

"Well, you see, it wouldn't stop with Wexler.

Once he starts talking, he won't quit. He'll tell me all about your conspiracy."

"Conspiracy!" Devlin said loudly. "You're out of your mind. There's no conspiracy."

Stillman looked skeptical. "I'm betting that Wexler will name names. Wanna call the bet?"

"What names?"

"Whoever you rigged into joining your game. There's greedy people everywhere, even Tenbow."

"Why would I do that?"

"You're a small-time grifter," Stillman said. "You saw the chance for a big play, but you needed financial backing. I think you put together a group here in town, men like Wexler. They supplied the funds and you fronted the operation."

Devlin was silent a moment. "For the sake of argument, let's say you're right. I still haven't broken any laws."

"That's for the courts to decide," Stillman said. "But it wouldn't matter one way or another. Once Wexler starts talking, your game's gone to hell. Nobody would sell you a square foot of land."

"No soap," Devlin said, shaking his head. "Wexler might talk, and then again he might not. I'll just have to take my chances."

"We're not talking chances," Stillman informed him. "We're talking choices. If Wexler won't talk, that leaves you the second choice I mentioned."

"Which is?"

"We'll have to settle our personal score."

"What personal score?"

"For openers," Stillman said, "you've been running around town calling me a liar. Then there's the matter of your friend"—he paused, indicating Johnson—"trying to backshoot me. I take all that real personal."

"So what?" Devlin suddenly looked worried. "You've got no proof."

"Don't need any," Stillman said in a cold voice. "I'll call you out and make you fight. Every man has his limits, even you."

"Jesus Christ, I don't even carry a gun!"

"Then I'd suggest you get one today."

Carl Richter cleared his throat. "There's another way," he interjected. "And it might work out better for all concerned. Devlin, let's suppose I offered to buy you out?"

"Try me," Devlin said shakily. "What kind of offer?"

"A fair one," Richter said. "All the land you've bought, I'll buy from you. And I'll add ten percent for your trouble."

"What about my partners?"

"So far as I'm concerned, Wexler and anybody else involved is a thief. Serve 'em right if you just take the money and run."

"And you end up with the land, is that it?"

"Tell you what," Richter said. "I'll donate it to the widows you stole it from. They can sell it to the railroad. Sound fair?"

"A bird in the hand," Devlin said with a sly smile. "You got yourself a deal."

Within the hour, the deeds were signed over and Richter rendered payment. A short while later Devlin and Johnson stepped aboard the noon stage, headed south. As the coach pulled away, Stillman and Richter shook hands. Then Richter gave him a curious look.

"Would you have killed them?"

"Probably not," Stillman admitted. "But Devlin wasn't too sure abut it."

"Tell you the truth, neither was I."

Stillman smiled. "Guess we'll never know."

EIGHTEEN

The inquest began the next morning. All of the concerned parties had been served notice by the sheriff's deputies the previous day. Their presence was required by law rather than being voluntary. To fail to appear would have resulted in an arrest warrant.

Proceedings were held in the county courtroom. Sheriff Lon Hubbard and two deputies were present, there to assist the coroner and maintain order. The spectator benches were filled with townspeople as well as several farmers and ranchers. Some of them had lost family in the killings, and others has lost friends. They wanted to hear the details of Joe Quinn's death.

Stillman and Carl Richter were seated in a front-row bench, directly before the empty jury box. Across the aisle, occupying the other front-row bench, were Amanda Sontag and Jud Holt. Since entering the courtroom, neither of them had so much as glanced in Stillman's direction. The spectators watched with avid interest, aware of the hostility on either side of the aisle. They awaited what promised to be a grim and sordid tale.

Dr. Alvin Phillips, the county coroner, emerged from the judge's chambers. A stir swept through the crowd, for they were reminded that the late Judge Taggart had been one of the murder victims. The sheriff called the proceedings to order and took a position before the jury box. Dr. Phillips settled himself in a chair behind the judge's bench and opened a folder filled with papers. At length he looked out across the packed courtroom.

"This is an official inquest," he said gravely. "By law the county coroner is empowered to inquire into the circumstances of an unusual or violent death. Today we will inquire into the death of one Joseph R. Quinn."

The spectators stared back at him with rapt attention. The entire town was aware that Joseph R. Quinn had been a brief resident of the local undertaker's funeral parlor. Yesterday, without ceremony or graveside services, he had been buried in a distant corner of Tenbow's cemetery.

"A note of caution," Phillips went on. "Anyone called to testify will be sworn and placed under oath. Just like a court trial, any witness who lies will be charged with perjury. The penalty for perjury in Wyoming Territory is two years in prison."

The first witness called was Carl Richter. Since the county prosecutor had also been murdered, Dr. Phillips assumed the role of interrogator. Under questioning, Richter explained the circumstances that had led to his hiring Jack Stillman. There were muffled snickers from the crowd when he commented that the sheriff seemed incapable of solving the murders. He further stated that Stillman had been hired as an investigator, not a bounty hunter. The purpose was to halt the killings and bring the killer to justice.

When Richter finished, Stillman took the witness stand. The coroner asked a few preliminary questions, then allowed Stillman to relate the details of his investigation in his own words. He recounted everything that had happened since his arrival in Tenbow. Some of the revelations, particularly those involving Devlin and Sontag, drew murmurs of anger from the spectators. He concluded with the final manhunt that had ended at Quinn's mountain camp. Given no choice, he had been forced to kill the fugitive.

"I have a few questions," Phillips said when

he finished. "Are you satisfied beyond any reasonable doubt that Joe Quinn committed all nine of these murders?"

"Yessir, I am," Stillman said firmly. "The motive was established, and the manner of the killings indicates that it was Quinn in each instance. I also recovered his rifle, and it was a .50-90 Sharps." He paused, glancing at Lon Hubbard. "The sheriff will verify that a Sharps was used in the killings."

Hubbard bobbed his head in solemn affirmation. Phillips looked at the sheriff, then his gaze shifted back to Stillman. "You've testified," he said, "that you wanted to capture Quinn, take him alive. Would you expound on your reasons?"

"That goes back five years," Stillman said. "Quinn was convicted of attempted rape and sentenced to prison. When he got out, he came back here and started killing people. One way or another, all of them had a hand in his conviction."

"By that you mean the judge, the prosecutor, and the jury?"

"And Will Sontag, because he's the one that pressed the charges."

"For the record," Phillips noted, "you're saying that Quinn's motive was revenge?"

"No doubt about it," Stillman said. "He was railroaded into prison and he meant to kill everyone involved. Before I caught up with him, he'd finished the job."

"What does that have to do with your efforts to take him alive?"

"Quinn didn't get justice the last time he was in this courtroom. Of course, he killed nine men and he'd likely have hanged for that. But I figured he deserved another day on the witness stand—to set the record straight."

Phillips appeared confused. "Are you talking about *why* he killed those men?"

"That's what this case was all about. Joe Quinn was framed and convicted on trumped-up charges. He should've had a chance to tell his side of the story—why he went on a killing spree."

"You state with some authority that Quinn was falsely accused and convicted. How can you be so certain of that?"

Stillman shrugged. "I got it straight from a woman who should know—Amanda Sontag."

The courtroom erupted in a buzz of conversation. Phillips took up the gavel and hammered the crowd into silence. After restoring order, he glowered down at Stillman. "That's a serious allegation you've made, Mr. Stillman. Are you prepared to substantiate it?"

"There's what's called 'a friend of the court.' Someone who's allowed to ask questions even though he's not an official. Let me question

Mrs. Sontag under oath and I think we'll get at the truth."

"That's highly irregular."

"Yessir, it is," Stillman agreed. "But there's more to it than Quinn's conviction on attempted rape. There are some unanswered questions about these murders."

"Such as?"

"Why cover the same ground twice? That's what I want to ask Mrs. Sontag."

Phillips deliberated for a long moment. At last he excused Stillman and called Amanda Sontag to the stand. Her features were pale and drawn, but she carried herself with stiff-backed pride. After she was sworn in, she sat down in the witness chair.

"All right, Mr. Stillman," Phillips said. "I'll allow you to act as a 'friend of the court.' But your questions better be addressed to the issue. Understand?"

"Yessir."

Stillman walked to the end of the jury box. He positioned himself so that everyone in the courtroom had a clear view of the witness stand. Amanda Sontag stared straight ahead, looking over and beyond the spellbound crowd. Her eyes were dull and lifeless.

"Mrs. Sontag," Stillman said gently, "I'm not out to embarrass you. But I think it's time we heard the truth—don't you?"

"Yes." Her voice was almost inaudible. "Ask whatever you want."

"The day your husband was killed, you told me he'd caught on about you and Quinn. What did you mean by that?"

"Joe Quinn and I were having an affair."

A woman in the crowd gasped. Stillman quickly went on. "What did your husband do after he found out?"

"Nothing, at first," she said. "He was afraid of Quinn, too scared to do anything himself. So he decided to bring charges on attempted rape."

"And you went along with the idea?"

"I had no choice. He would have turned me out if I hadn't agreed. Besides, after he'd brought charges, I couldn't humiliate him. I had to go along."

"Let's get it straight," Stillman said. "Your choice was to humiliate your husband or send Joe Quinn to prison. So you lied under oath and got Quinn convicted. Isn't that how it happened?"

"Yes," she said softly. "I did what my husband told me to do."

"And sent an innocent man to prison?"

"Yes."

"All right," Stillman said, "let's skip ahead five years. Quinn got out of prison last spring and came back to the valley. Only you and your husband knew he'd returned. How'd you find out?"

"One morning—" Her voice broke, and she took a moment to collect herself. "After the men had ridden out to work, Joe snuck into the house. He told me what he intended to do—kill everyone."

"Everyone involved with his conviction?"

She nodded. "He said he meant to save my husband for last. He wanted Will to die a little bit each day."

"The day he came to your house, was that before he'd killed anybody?"

"Yes . . . a week before."

"A week before the first killing," Stillman said. "So you and your husband had time to notify the sheriff?"

She bowed her head. "Will wouldn't even discuss it. He was afraid someone would discover the truth." She looked up, her eyes distant. "How we'd convicted an innocent man."

"In other words, you did nothing while men were being killed one by one?"

"Not entirely," she said. "My husband sent for Jud—Jud Holt—even before the first murder. He was convinced Jud could track down Quinn and . . . stop him."

"Stop him?" Stillman asked. "Or kill him?"

"I suppose it amounts to the same thing."

"When Holt failed to find Quinn—and people were still being killed—was there any talk of going to the sheriff?"

"I tried," she said quietly. "But my husband wouldn't hear of it. He believed Jud would put an end to it."

"End the killing," Stillman said, "or end the threat to your husband? Which one do you mean?"

"Will only cared about himself. He never gave a thought to those other men."

"How much did he pay Holt for the job?"

"A thousand dollars. Half in advance and half when he'd . . . finished."

"And instead it was your husband that got finished?"

"Yes."

"One last question," Stillman said. "You were just as responsible as your husband for Quinn going to prison. Why didn't he kill you?"

"He loved me," she said, staring at nothing. "He knew Will had forced me to testify against him. Even after he got out of prison, he still loved me."

Stillman indicated that he had no more questions. Amanda Sontag was excused from the stand and walked slowly back to her seat. The spectators watched her with a mixture of loathing and pity, as though a leper had appeared in their midst. Yet even in the moment of her public shame, she had gained some small sense of atonement. Her guilt was no longer so hard to bear.

There were no other witnesses. Phillips saw nothing to be achieved in calling Jud Holt to the stand. All that was relevant to the case had been told, with greater clarity than anyone might have imagined. Perhaps the most revealing fact uncovered was how Will Sontag had learned that a killer was stalking the valley. To the crowd, the sordid affair between Quinn and the Sontag woman simply confirmed her loose reputation. The testimony somehow absolved a man who had killed in his quest of retribution.

Phillips made a short statement. He commended Stillman for righting an old wrong as well as putting himself at risk to halt the killings. He next delivered a heated commentary about the treachery some men imposed on other men, and how it should serve as a lesson for all who lived in Tenbow Valley. Then, slamming the gavel down, he rendered his decision:

"The death of Joseph R. Quinn is hereby ruled justifiable homicide."

Outside the courthouse, Stillman and Richter started down the walkway. For different reasons they were both pleased with the outcome of the inquest. Richter saw it as the end to a case that had made neighbor suspicious of neighbor. Stillman felt there had been vindication of a good man gone bad, justice served for all concerned. The tenth dead man, Joe Quinn, would now rest easier.

"Stillman!"

A harsh voice brought them around. Jud Holt hurried down the walkway, his face set in a disgruntled scowl. Behind him, surrounded by the crowd of spectators, Amanda Sontag waited on the courthouse steps. Holt slowed as he approached the two men, his eyes burning with fury. He halted a couple of paces away, directly in front of Stillman.

"Goddamn you!" he said coarsely. "You couldn't leave it alone, could you?"

"Leave what alone?"

"You made a fool out of me with the International. They all knew I'd been hired to protect Sontag. I'll probably never work for the Association again!"

Stillman frowned. "You blame me for that?"

"Who the hell else?" Holt grated. "We could've worked together if you'd treated me square. But no, you had to grab all the glory for yourself."

"Not much glory in killing a man."

"Don't try to weasel out of it! You should've told me who you were."

"I work alone," Stillman said. "Besides, you'd been on the case a month when I got here. Wasn't like I walked in and stole your thunder."

Holt's mouth tightened. "What about today? You and your goddamn inquest made me look like a nitwit. And you all but labeled Amanda a whore!"

"Way it looked to me, she wanted to testify. She had a lot to get off her mind."

"Sonovabitch, you got a way with words, don't you? Well, I'm done talkin'! We're gonna settle this here and now."

"Simmer down," Stillman said. "You've impressed you lady friend and the crowd. Let's drop it there."

Holt glared at him. "You refusin' to fight?"

"Jud, I'd sooner walk away than kill you. Don't push your luck."

Stillman turned, with Richter at his side, and started across the street. As they approached the opposite corner, a woman screamed from the courthouse steps. An instant later a slug whistled past Stillman and the report of a gunshot echoed through town. He whirled around, drawing his Colt, and saw Holt thumbing the hammer for another shot. There was a look of frenzied desperation on Holt's features.

The second slug clipped a lamppost on the corner. Stillman brought his pistol to shoulder level, mentally calculating the distance at twenty paces. He steadied the sights on Holt's chest and fired. A starburst of blood appeared on Holt's shirt and he lurched backward. Then, arms windmilling, he staggered off the walkway and fell on the courthouse lawn. His right leg twitched in a spasm of afterdeath.

Stillman lowered his pistol. He sensed Richter watching him and saw the sheriff push through the crowd on the courthouse steps. His gaze shifted to Amanda Sontag and their eyes locked. He shook his head, almost in apology, but there was no response. Her face was void of emotion.

He turned downtown, suddenly weary of the killing.

By noontime Stillman's business was concluded in Tenbow. With dozens of eyewitnesses to the shooting, the sheriff saw no need for a formal hearing. Jud Holt had fired first, an assassin's attack from behind. Stillman had defended himself, responding to the threat in a lawful manner. The case was duly and swiftly closed.

Carl Richter settled accounts with similar speed. He stepped into the bank and returned with a thousand dollars in cash. The sum exceeded what he owed Stillman, but he declared that twenty dollars a day was insufficient for the job performed. Several people, he noted, had tried to kill Stillman, and hazard alone dictated a bonus. Outside the hotel they parted with a warm handshake just before Richter mounted his horse. Neither of them was sorry to see the assignment ended.

There was one piece of unfinished business. Stillman crossed the street, angling toward the Tivoli. When he entered, the noonday crowd went silent with respect, watching as he walked past the bar. Upstairs, he moved down a hallway and stopped before one of several doors. He rapped lightly with his knuckles.

Jennie opened the door. She wore a sheer peignoir loosely belted at the waist. Her room was poorly furnished, typical of a saloon girl who lived one day to the next. Yet her smile was bright and vivacious, and her little squeal of happiness was genuine. Grabbing him, she pulled him into the room and kicked the door shut. She peppered his face with kisses.

"God, I'm glad to see you! How'd the inquest go?"

Stillman knew she seldom awoke before noon. From her question she'd heard nothing of the courthouse gunfight, and he decided to leave it that way. "Worked out fine," he said. "I'm through with the case."

"Ummm, good," she purred. "Now we'll have some time to ourselves."

"Let me ask you something," Stillman said, detaching himself from her arms. "An honest answer to an honest question, fair enough?"

"Why sure, sugar. What is it?"

Stillman was fairly certain of the answer. He tried to couch the question in a tactful manner. "Suppose you could leave Tenbow today?" he said. "Where would you want to go?"

"I dunno—"

"C'mon, give me an honest answer."

"Well . . ." she hesitated, then laughed. "San Francisco! Every girl that comes west wants to see Frisco."

There were a thousand like her, girls stranded on their way to somewhere else. Sooner or later they all began to dream of the city by the bay. "No fibs now," Stillman persisted. "You'd choose Frisco with or without me—wouldn't you?"

"Jeez," she said softly, "you're putting me on the spot."

"I think you just answered my question."

Stillman pulled out his bankroll. He peeled off five hundred dollars and pressed the bills into her hand. "There's your stake," he said, squeezing her hand closed. "That'll take you to Frisco in style."

She stared at the money. "What about you?"

"I'm headed back to Cheyenne."

"Oh." She gave him a look of infinite wisdom. "What's her name, the girl in Cheyenne?"

Stillman smiled. "Her name's Laura."

"Well, you're a sweet man, sugar. The sweetest man I ever met. Tell Laura I said so."

She threw her arms around him in a tight embrace. When they parted, her eyes were misty and neither of them could think of anything to say. She smiled bravely, clutching the money to her breast, as he moved across the room. Then the door opened and closed, and he was gone.

An hour later, Stillman reined to a halt on the road south of town. He twisted around in the saddle and sat for a moment staring at Tenbow. The thing he would remember most was not the manhunt or the girl, or even his brush with death. What stuck in his mind instead was perhaps the oddest aspect of the case. Joe Quinn and Jud Holt, for all their differences, had proved to be very much alike. There was a certain irony to it, but it was nonetheless true. Some men lived out their lives waiting to be killed.

Stillman reined away from Tenbow. The distant mountains stood washed in sunlight as he nudged his bay into a trot. He rode south toward Cheyenne.

READ THESE MASTERFUL WESTERNS BY MATT BRAUN

"Matt Braun is a master storyteller of frontier history."
—Elmer Kelton

THE KINCAIDS

Golden Spur Award-winner THE KINCAIDS tells the classic saga of America at its most adventurous through the eyes of three generations who made laws, broke laws, and became legends in their time.

GENTLEMAN ROGUE

Hell's Half Acre is Fort Worth's violent ghetto of whore-houses, gaming dives and whisky wells. And for shootist and gambler Luke Short, it's a place to make a stand. But he'll have to stake his claim from behind the barrel of a loaded gun . . .

RIO GRANDE

Tom Stuart, a hard-drinking, fast-talking steamboat captain, has a dream of building a shipping empire that will span the Gulf of Mexico to New Orleans. Now, Stuart is plunged into the fight of a lifetime—and to the winner will go the mighty Rio Grande . . .

THE BRANNOCKS

The three Brannock brothers were reunited in a boomtown called Denver. And on a frontier brimming with opportunity and exploding with danger, vicious enemies would test their courage—and three beautiful women would claim their love . . .

America's Authentic Voice of the Western Frontier

Matt Braun

Bestselling author of *Bloody Hand*

HICKOK & CODY

In the wind-swept campsite of the Fifth Cavalry Regiment, along Red Willow Creek, Russia's Grand Duke Alexis has arrived to experience the thrill of the buffalo hunt. His guides are: Wild Bill Hickok and Buffalo Bill Cody—two heroic dead-shots with a natural flair for showmanship, a hunger for adventure, and the fervent desire to keep the myths of the Old West alive. But what approached from the East was a journey that crossed the line into dangerous territory. It would offer Alexis a front row seat to history, and would set Hickok and Cody on a path to glory.

"Braun tackles the big men, the complex personalities of those brave few who were pivotal figures in the settling of an untamed frontier."
—Jory Sherman, author of *Grass Kingdom*

"Matt Braun has a genius for taking real characters out of the Old West and giving them flesh-and-blood immediacy."
—Dee Brown, author of *Bury My Heart at Wounded Knee*

AVAILABLE WHEREVER BOOKS ARE SOLD
FROM ST. MARTIN'S PAPERBACKS

HC 8/02

For decades the Texas plains ran with the blood of natives and settlers, as pioneers carved out ranch land from ancient Indian hunting grounds and the U.S. Army turned the tide of battle. Now the Civil War has begun, and the Army is pulling out of Fort Belknap—giving the Comanches a new chance for victory and revenge.

Led by the remarkable warrior, Little Buffalo, the Comanche and Kiowa are united in a campaign to wipe out the settlers forever. But in their way stand two remarkable men . . .

Allan Johnson is a former plantation owner. Britt Johnson was once his family slave, now a freed man facing a new kind of hatred on the frontier. Together, with a rag-tag volunteer army, they'll stand up for their hopes and dreams in a journey of courage and conscience that will lead to victory . . . or death.

Black Fox

A NOVEL BY

Matt Braun

BESTSELLING AUTHOR OF
Wyatt Earp